Louis Dantin

"When after my death this manuscript is found, dated on the final page, people will perhaps say to themselves, 'You see, he finished this tale of his youth at seventy-eight, or eighty!' Or else they will find it unfinished and will see then that there are some things which one feels so strongly that it is almost impossible to express them."

These words are taken from a letter which Louis Dantin wrote to me on March 12, 1942. Eventually he found the time and the energy to finish the novel to which he had dedicated himself for so long. The final chapters were written or dictated to me by the author during a time when the blindness which was to become total a short while before his death was beginning to afflict him.

Louis Dantin was a man of rare delicacy of mind and heart. He was loath to offend even his enemies. Because of the autobiographical nature of this book, he feared that its publication during his lifetime would be cause for scandal. It was this scruple which kept him from offering it to the public. Only once did he show signs of a change of feeling — at a time when his relationship with Haitian poets seemed to make publication easier. He wrote me then: "Do you know what preposterous idea has come into my head? To publish *Les Enfances de Fanny* in serial form in a Haitian newspaper. Recently a Haiti-Canada committee was formed to encourage an exchange between

1

the two literatures. I wonder if *Fanny* would not as well as any other work provide such a link."

To Doctor Gabriel Nadeau, one of his most intimate friends and author of the remarkable book, *Louis Dantin, sa vie et son oeuvre* (Éditions Lafayette, Manchester, N.H., 1948), he confided with regret during the course of their innumerable conversations: "The book will never see the light of day; it would cause a scandal. Look at the storm raised by Lillian Smith's novel (*Strange Fruit*). That book, however, is concerned with less burning issues, and furthermore the author's personality is not involved in it, while *Fanny* is a piece of my life; it is the remembrance of a period when I was in great distress, not knowing which way to turn, when I sought affection as a beggar asks for bread. I braved all the world's conventions then and I do not blush today because of that attachment: a human sentiment belongs to humanity. *Fanny* is a debt of gratitude. In paying it I have taken the final step toward divesting myself and laying bare my heart."

In offering *Les Enfances de Fanny* today I in turn am paying a debt of gratitude to Louis Dantin. I am fulfilling his ardent, oft-expressed desire to see his book printed after his death. It was to this end that he made me legatee of the manuscript. At the same time, this publication completes the work of one of our most authentic intellectuals, who was the friend and mentor of most of his contemporaries.

It will perhaps be said that this book adds but little to Louis Dantin's literary value. But it is in fact no less precious a document for the study of the author's personality than a statement of his attitude toward all human injustice.

It would be presumptuous to want to present Louis

Dantin to today's educated public. He is still too much alive in our hearts and memories. Introduced to our literature by his masterful preface to Nelligan's work, Dantin was a delicate storyteller and showed great powers of observation in *La vie en rêve*. He was the skilful bard of *Coffret de Crusoé* and the grand poet of *Chanson intellectuelle*. Above all, he was one of our best critics. Living in anonymity for over a quarter of a century, first in Cambridge, then in Boston, he painstakingly studied almost the entire literary output of French Canada, giving the authors encouragement and sage counsel.

An extremely severe childhood, devoted almost exclusively to study and devoid of the games and diversions of those his own age; a tormented adolescence spent in Paris, Rome, Brussels, Montreal; his first contact with love; his slow and painful separation from his early religious beliefs; his voluntary exile; the cruel abandonment by one beloved; his bitter and desperate struggle to make a living, his confinement in the austere Harvard University Press — these were the forces of destiny which fashioned this figure, enigmatic to the stranger but of great simplicity to one who knew him, the humane, just figure that was Louis Dantin.

It was at Cambridge, and later at Roxbury — Boston's "little Africa" — among black people that Dantin found the sympathy and affection for which he so passionately thirsted. It was black people who spoke consoling words to him; it was there among them that his upright heart revolted against the crime of segregation of black and white. It is this period of his life of which, in part, this novel speaks.

R. Dion-Levesque

3

THE "FRENCH WRITERS OF CANADA" SERIES

The purpose of this series is to bring to English readers, for the first time, in a uniform and inexpensive format, a selection of outstanding and representative works of fiction by French authors in Canada. Individual titles in the series will range from the most modern work to the classic. Our editors have examined the entire repertory of French fiction in this country to ensure that each book that is selected will reflect important literary and social trends, in addition to having evident aesthetic value.

Current Titles in the Series

Ethel and the Terrorist, a novel by Claude Jasmin, translated by David Walker.

The Temple on the River, a novel by Jacques Hébert, translated by Gerald Taaffe.

Ashini, a novel by Yves Thériault, translated by Gwendolyn Moore.

N'Tsuk, a novel by Yves Thériault, translated by Gwendolyn Moore.

The Torrent, novellas and short stories by Anne Hébert, translated by Gwendolyn Moore.

Dr. Cotnoir, a novel by Jacques Ferron, translated by Pierre Cloutier.

Fanny, a novel by Louis Dantin, translated by Raymond Chamberlain (winter 1974).

The Saint Elias, a novel by Jacques Ferron, translated by Pierre Cloutier (spring 1974).

The Juneberry Tree, a novel by Jacques Ferron (forthcoming).

Jos Carbone, a novel by Jacques Benoit (forthcoming).

The Grandfathers, a novel by Victor-Lévy Beaulieu (forthcoming).

Fanny

a novel by
Louis Dantin

translated by
Raymond Y. Chamberlain

Advisory Editors
Ben-Zion Shek and Réjean Robidoux,
Department of French,
University of Toronto

Copyright © 1973, 1974 by Harvest House Ltd.
All rights reserved.
Library of Congress Catalog Card No. 73-85498
ISBN 88772 143 5
Deposited in the Bibliothèque Nationale of
Québec
1st quarter, 1974.
Originally published in the French language
by Le Cercle du Livre de France Ltée,
Montreal, as *Les Enfances de Fanny*.

For information address Harvest House Ltd.
4795 St. Catherine St. W., Montreal,
Quebec, H3Z 2B9

Printed and bound in Canada.

Designed by Robert Reid
Cover illustration by Allan Harrison

The Publishers gratefully acknowledge a
publication grant from the Canada Council.

6

FANNY

I

Fanny had just come into the cabin in tears; her elder sister, who looked after her and acted as her guardian, had caught her climbing trees with a group of boys and had spanked her.

"Shame on you" her sister cried angrily, still holding her by the ear. "When will you learn that you're a girl and that you've got to behave like one? My back is scarcely turned before you take off to run in the fields with those dirty little brats, jumping over chicken roosts, chasing after the cow and the hens, knocking down cornstalks, trampling on my flower beds. Just look at that dress, blacker than your face. I put it on you this morning perfectly clean. Why does the Lord burden me with the harsh cross of such a child? Perhaps next time you'll understand that strap on the wall better!"

The guilty one lowered her head and excused herself contritely: "Charlie Ross was after me," she said; "he wanted to beat me up. So I climbed . . ."

"The devil's after you, young lady, and he'll get you if you don't watch out. Take note that it's written in the Holy Book, since it's your good fortune to be able to read. Now go wash off that filth and get straight to your lessons. Mr. Lewis told me again yesterday that your schoolwork was none too good."

This scene occurred in Virginia, in a run-down cabin in the village of Greenway, where the two Negro sisters lived — Linda, a widow in her thirties, and

Fanny, just turned twelve. Their maternal grandmother had been a slave, the favorite slave, it was said, of the planter Johnston, which no doubt explained why both had delicate brown complexions and thinner, more refined features than are commonly found in their race. They led a meager existence, keeping a few hens and farming a tiny piece of land; they had a pig which was fed on table scraps and a cow which grazed along the side of the road and spent the winter in a neighbor's shed. Linda also worked by the day in the homes of white families in the area.

No two personalities could have been more different than those of the two sisters. The elder, naturally serious, had acquired an austere, puritanical mind from the sermons that she so often attended and the frenzied exhortations of revivalists. Religion ruled her thoughts. She saw the devil everywhere and spirituals thundered in her ear, telling of the crossing of the Jordan, the armies of the Lord sweeping over the earth, the horror of Judgment Day, the final defeat of the sinners. Anything joyful — music, dancing, singing, love — especially love — seemed to her Satan's trap, and she was determined that the young sister confided to her care be raised on the same principles.

But in Fanny's veins there ran the exuberant sap of the jungle. A fiery youngster, alert, forever on the move, driven by wild and daring instincts, all she wanted to do was race through the woods or tumble about in the grass. Stronger and more agile than any of the boys, she joined in their rough games, more than once pummeling the same Charlie Ross whom she pretended to fear. Her escapades landed her in all sorts of predicaments. She slipped off the roof

10

of the pigsty where only the muddy earth saved her; she fell into the well, and one evening a bull chased her along a fence that she cleared just in time. But a few good scares were nothing to her; lured by other adventures, she soon forgot them.

Her big sister and Mr. Lewis were the only two people who commanded her respect. It was for them alone that she felt sad when she thought of her great faults; only they could bring her to resist her own nature, however fleetingly and inadequately. She feared and venerated them as superior beings whom she had to appease in order to stay in their good graces. She loved them also with the heart of a young girl, eager for attachment, seeing in them the mother and father whom she had lost.

Mr. Lewis was her teacher; she had to appear before him each day to account for her poorly-learned lessons. He was a young man still, thirty-two, perhaps. Only recently arrived in the village, he took his job there seriously. Having overcome a thousand obstacles to get a decent education himself, he had the ambition to pass it on to others of his race. He labored conscientiously, teaching the small ones how to spell, guiding their awkward hands through the ink splotches. He made the more advanced ones read the Bible and taught them Methodist hymns along with arithmetic and United Sates history. Fanny put his patience to a severe test, though he discovered that in spite of her idleness she caught up with the rest because of her quick mind, to which grammar and numbers only offered other kinds of fences to jump; often, almost in spite of himself, he was forced to award her the highest grades and, at the same time, to forgive her a great deal of mischief.

He had noticed the astonishingly pure tone of her

voice and had let her into the choir that he directed for church services, and seeing her always ready to gallivant through the streets, he used her to run errands for the school. The child felt proud of these privileges and her devotion to Mr. Lewis grew to the point of idolatry. She would have liked to be diligent and well-behaved for him, but out of school her awakened senses would take hold of her once more and again she would find herself running in the fields, plundering birds' nests, decimating strawberry patches, pulling down cherries in the company of roughnecks of whom she seemed to be the queen. Yet, in other ways she was as naive as a new-born baby, ignorant of carnal instincts and the facts of life, still believing in the beneficent role of the stork.

II

She reached thirteen, then fourteen, without any apparent changes in her life. But her figure was rapidly becoming slender, her bust molding itself into gracious roundness. Unsuspectingly, the tomboy was turning into a young girl and her indecisive prettiness was beginning to show a budding beauty. The boys, with whom she played as before, looked at her strangely from time to time, and one day at the high point of a battle between her and Charlie Ross, the latter succeeded in throwing her down; then, using all his strength to keep her on the ground, he kissed her squarely on each cheek. Furious, she bounded up right away and gave him the worst beating he had ever received. But their companions had seen it all and made fun of it, chanting "Charlie Ross kissed Fanny!" The fact was noised about, embellished with details by the hero's boasting. A gossip thought it her duty to inform the elder sister. "Do you know what they're saying, Miss Linda? That your Fanny lets herself be kissed by that bum of a Charlie Ross."

The good woman's indignation was beyond words. The scandal put the crowning touch on Fanny's excesses; it deserved terrible punishment. In vain the girl insisted upon her abused innocence and the vengeance that she had reaped.

"How did I know what he was going to do? And I beat one of his eyes to a pulp, didn't I?"

"Little hellion!" Linda kept saying. "That's where your evil bent leads you — your disobedience to the holy laws. I ought to whip you till you scream for mercy, but you don't care any more about getting spanked than you do about getting bawled out. What can I do? I have one last resort; somebody has to help me. I'm going to tell Mr. Lewis everything."

"No, no, Linda, don't do that! I give you my word, I won't play with them again!"

But Linda knew such promises and was unrelenting; Mr. Lewis received the deplorable news that same day. It surprised him greatly, for the little demon that he knew had always appeared to him as a ray of complete purity; he could not imagine her involved, even slightly, with the vulgar world of the senses, and this discovery left him oddly disturbed and with a feeling of almost personal sorrow. He found it appalling to imagine that boy pressing his gross lips against Fanny's fresh cheeks, and maybe against her mouth; it seemed a sacrilege.

"This is outrageous!" he said. "But send the little one to me; I'll speak to her."

"Mr. Lewis wants to speak to you," said Linda dryly, when she returned home, to the child she had left protesting with rage. "He'll wait for you after school."

"I won't go! I won't go!" Fanny said over and over. But she knew that she would go and that she would have to swallow her shame and disgrace in front of her idol; the thought tormented her.

All night she tossed upon her folding cot, assailed in her sleeplessness by strange reflections. Why, indeed, had Charlie Ross kissed her? Why do people kiss? She recalled now that in spite of her anger the light brush against her cheek had seemed agreeable to her. But what right did he have to insult her so? What she resented more than anything else was that he had condemned her to Mr. Lewis' scorn. What would her teacher think of her? Would he smile from now on when he met her? Would he let her carry his packages and deliver his messages? How forlorn she would feel, isolated, rejected by her great friend! For he would no longer believe her and would refuse to accept her excuses.

The morning class was interminable. The teacher refrained from asking her any questions and that seemed a bad omen. When the students had filed out she saw him start with a grave air towards the bench where she sat riveted and alone. She arose as he drew near, stiff with embarrassment.

"Fanny," he began, "bad things are being said about you. Is it true that you are free with boys, that Charlie Ross kisses you?"

She had thought of answers and explanations, but suddenly a veil was drawn across her mind; she could no longer find anything to say.

"I wouldn't have believed it of you," the teacher continued. "You're undisciplined enough in class and negligent enough with your lessons without it coming to that sort of thing. I was trying to help you; I believed that you wanted to please me and you make a fool of me? People think I'm soft on you. They're going to ridicule me. 'Look how his little pet acts!' they'll say. Really, is that very nice? Answer me."

This unforeseen appeal to her affection for her teacher suddenly opened the floodgates. Shaken by sobs and her cheeks wet with piteous tears, she confided in her teacher:

"Yes, it's true, he kissed me, just one time, no, twice, but he took me by force. We were playing; I'm usually stronger than he is, but that time he knocked me down. Mr. Lewis, I promise you I didn't want to. And right then I started to beat him, and I beat him till his nose was bloody. You'll see at the next class how his face is still swollen. I want to please you, Mr. Lewis, and I'm not lying to you!"

"Then you're doing nothing wrong with those kids? You're not fond of Charlie Ross?"

"Charlie Ross? Me?" Choked, and not knowing what to say, she spat on the floor several times. She was almost beautiful, anger aroused, eyes flashing. Mr. Lewis was touched.

"Well, I want to believe you. But you see what a person gets for hanging around those scoundrels. After this will you stay away from Charlie Ross and his gang?"

"I don't want to see them any more, I hate all of them. I'll study, I'll run your errands for you. I'll be well-behaved, Mr. Lewis! I promise."

"Then don't cry any longer. We'll forget all about

15

it. Just remember what you have promised me."

But the flow of tears took time to run dry. Though still upset, Fanny had raised her eyes. She was looking at Mr. Lewis and adoration shone through her tears.

He drew her to him paternally, enclosing the quivering child in his arms. Then, carried away by the desire to console her and haunted without knowing it, perhaps, by the other caress that she had suffered, with a spontaneous, almost unconscious gesture he pressed his cheek softly against hers.

"Here, you see, I don't blame you."

And even as she cried Fanny started to laugh, nervously, ecstatically. Her laugh, like her voice, was extraordinary. It had the tone of a tinkling bell, the ring of crystal, the clear babble of a spring. She was laughing happily now, sure of his forgiveness.

Moved, Mr. Lewis listened to the laughter unfold and its silver notes charmed his ear.

It was with a light step that Fanny started back down the road leading to the cabin. Every detail, every word of the meeting sang in her memory. Mr. Lewis had been good to her; he had taken her word. And there was the miracle — she gasped just to think of it — he had embraced her! She could still feel the soft, affectionate touch of the teacher's cheek on hers, softer by far than Charlie Ross'.

But what would she say to Linda? Of course she could not tell her what had happened. Something told her that this happiness belonged only to her, that a secret had passed between her and Mr. Lewis; so she assumed a sorrowful look to go along with her reddened eyes.

"Well?" demanded her sister, upon seeing her.

"Mister Lewis was very angry. He scolded me.

I promised to do better."

"Amen. But we'll see."

III

But Fanny surprised everyone by giving up her wild ways, at least the wildest of them. From that day she ceased to play with the boys and to climb trees, and when she went running in the fields she went alone or with harmless infants tagging along behind her. She spent her excess energies hoeing the garden and cleaning the hen-house or doing the laundry with stubborn dedication. In class, especially, she was transformed. She was no longer seen setting loose June bugs or tossing marbles under the tables or pinching her neighbors. She kept her eyes fixed on her book or more often still, on the lips and movements of Mr. Lewis. Her former companions could not understand it.

"Turning against your old friends?" asked Charlie Ross, meeting her as she was leaving school.

"I don't like disrespectful boys," she replied, with her nose held high.

"What! If I kissed you, it probably wasn't because I hate you."

"I don't care if you hate me or not; I just want you to leave me alone."

"Got some other friends, then?"

"Maybe. But what's it to you?"

"Nothing. Only look out if I catch you by yourself; I'll kiss you again anyway."

"Oh, no you won't; you'll be dead first."

Mr. Lewis was delighted with his success and felt almost grateful towards the child. His interest in her grew steadily, but, at the same time, in the presence of the other students, he wore a mask of indifference. Although seeming to have less to do with her, he had persuaded Linda to let her come each evening to dust and sweep the school. This allowed him to talk with her and continue to advise her. Meanwhile, he helped her rehearse for the solos that she sang at church. Then, he found occasion to visit the two sisters and sometimes Linda would ask him to supper with Fanny serving them. Those hours, surrounded by the lavish attentions of his hostesses, by the laughter and chatter of the younger one, were extremely pleasant ones for him.

As for Fanny, Mr. Lewis' friendship enchanted her; she gave herself up to it as to a splendid wave. She hastened to anticipate his smallest desires and looked for ways to serve him personally, such as stealing his handkerchiefs to wash them or sharpening his pencils in his absence; she shared with him the smallest details of her life, becoming almost familiar. Now and then, finding him absorbed in correcting exercises, she would startle him by entering with a shout or deliberately overturning a bench, and she hid behind desks so as to leap out in front of him and take a bow. The teacher smiled at her childish behavior.

But little by little an obsession took hold of Fanny's mind. Why the dignified reserve that he maintained? He had not even repeated the timid caress that he had given her. At long intervals, a friendly pat — that was all she was granted in return for her sacrifices. He acted as though he were afraid of her, seeming to seek her out and to flee from her at the same time. She suffered greatly from such coldness and there was a mystery to it that she wanted to penetrate.

One day she said straightforwardly, "Mr. Lewis, I'm going to start being a bad girl again."

"Hold on! What's that you're saying?" exclaimed the teacher.

"Yes, you have a lot more fun. You run and jump whenever you feel like it. You have a good time with boys. I like to play with them; they're strong and adventurous. Charlie Ross wants me to come back with them. If he's just looking to kiss me, well, I'll beat him up again."

"You're kidding, aren't you, little idiot? Then you're tired of being good, of working for me and pleasing your big sister?"

"It's not that, Mr. Lewis, but you, you don't like me very much; really now, I can see that. You're always serious — you don't laugh with me. Sometimes I'm bored."

Fanny had wanted to raise a storm and she had succeeded. Mr. Lewis felt a long-repressed tenderness flow into his heart. If the child only knew that his apparent coldness was only designed to conceal a torturing and secret love. At last it was clear to him; he had cherished her since the day that he had saved her from Charlie Ross. That caress given in an unguarded moment had tormented his memory often. He had feigned dignity with effort and restrained himself from sharing the laughter and gaiety of his pupil, and now she held it against him! She thought of looking elsewhere for hearts closer to her own! The idea of losing her, of letting her go back to her old friends seemed terrible and absurd.

"Fanny," he said, "you don't understand me. I do like you — very much; you're my very dear girl. You won't leave me, will you? Come, I won't be so serious any longer; I'll laugh as hard as you."

He had brought her close to him, and putting his arms around her as if to prevent her escape, deliberately, this time, he kissed her on both cheeks. Then Fanny threw her arms around his neck and among peals of laughter she moved across Mr. Lewis' captive face with her warm lips.

IV

They began an unusual adventure then, one full of exciting moments, but of worry and danger as well. Above all, they had to keep their secret, to prevent the pupils, and Linda especially, from discovering how close they had become; so they resorted to one ruse after another to avoid suspicion. In class Mr. Lewis pretended to be severe with Fanny, though she never did the extra lessons he assigned her, and they used the times that she was kept after school to be alone together. When he visited her at home he appeared to neglect her, giving all his attention to Linda; but even in front of her they passed notes to each other which, because she was unable to read, she thought was schoolwork. On holidays they met in remote corners of the countryside. There the high-spirited child would become herself again, running about gaily with her hair in the wind, gathering wild berries, trailing her feet in streams as much as she liked.

Although they were thrown together so much they only exchanged innocent caresses. Mr. Lewis had a conscience. The child had captivated him, she had become necessary to his life, but he respected her and felt repugnance at the thought of harming her. So the struggle continued within him between his quite human passion and the moral mission he had given himself. On her side, for all her playfulness, Fanny remained aware of the distance which separated her from her teacher. She felt that she was his queen and was proud to have conquered him, but he was still the teacher who knew so many things, the judge whom a host of children held in awe and who could praise her and punish her. While treating him like a favorite toy she revered him as a god.

"When we're alone," he told her, "you could call me by my first name."

"What, me call you Edward?" she replied, amused and surprised. "Oh, that would sound so funny. But, let's see, I'll try: I don't know my lesson, Edward. I like you a lot, Edward. No, no, Mr. Lewis, that would never do." She laughed, looking at him all the while with infinite respect.

But they allowed their need to be together to grow, and suffered from the many hours spent apart; until one day, with an air of indifference, Fanny approached her sister and said: "Linda, Mr. Lewis wants to know if you would like him to board here. He thinks his room is too far from school; it makes him lose time."

The proposition pleased the courageous widow right away. In poor Southern families a boarder is

21

always a blessing. And then, the teacher had such a healthy influence on Fanny.

"Tell Mr. Lewis," she answered, "that it will be a pleasure."

He came to stay at the cabin, so that he could be at his young friend's side. No longer was there any need for so many secret intrigues; Linda was often absent, so they were left alone for hours, whole days sometimes. Spoiled by the two sisters, adored by one of them, Mr. Lewis let himself be lulled in the comfort of a tranquil domestic life. Having Fanny always with him, his affection for her, though not diminished, became less intense, satisfied with milder pleasures. Calmly happy, he settled down to his good fortune.

Meanwhile winter passed. Then without warning, the hot, resplendent Virginia spring burst upon them, a time when Fanny was accustomed to go wandering, roaming the woods swollen with sap and full of thrilling odors. Now and then the desire for adventure came back to trouble her; vague regrets arose in her heart when, from her window she saw the outspread slopes inviting her to run madly across them, and Charlie Ross' gang rushing by on their way to rob nests.

But deep within her, other, obscure forces were awakening — ill-defined desires, feverish longings that had lain unnoticed, which made her dream of adventures and unknown joys that even her love for Mr. Lewis had left floating in mystery.

On one of those vibrant, electric days, the cabin bathed in breezes and bright sunlight, they had stayed home, alone together. The teacher was seated at a rickety table correcting schoolwork from the previous day. Fanny was busy cleaning and sang as she moved from place to place. She sang an old song

22

into which her fresh, clear voice put metallic into-
nations:

My grandfather's clock was too large for the shelf,

So it stood ninety years on the floor;
It was taller by half than the old man himself,
Though it weighed not a pennyweight more,
It was bought on the morn of the day that he was born,
And was always his treasure and pride;
But it stopped short — never to go again —
When the old man died.

Ninety years without slumbering (tick-tock,
                                         tick-tock),
His life seconds numbering (tick-tock, tick-tock).

But she was nervous, agitated; something would
not allow her to be still, and she was full of ca-
prices. She would have liked the roof to fly away
and to take her with it into the warm, blue sky. She
would have liked to dance without restraint in
some enchanted field, and to have Mr. Lewis dance
with her and roll with her in the grass and moss.
But he was correcting his exercises. Each time she
went near him she would disturb him with some prank
or other, but he would simply say: "Look, Fanny, be
good. You see I'm working." And she would move
away, impatient, as though struggling to free herself from invisible chains. Even the "tick-tock" of
her song bound her in its inexorable rhythm.

Little by little a feeling of rebellion took hold of
her. She had to break the silent, oppressive calm at
any cost. She sought some daring act which would
liberate her and arouse Mr. Lewis, force him, whether
he liked it or not, to pay attention to her. Absently

23

she arranged her room and remade her bed, keeping her eyes on him, trembling nervously at what she was about to do. Suddenly, she grabbed one of her pillows and threw it with all her might at his head, and before he could turn around, the other pillow struck him, spilling its stuffing. Next, one after the other, sheets and blankets flew, burying him beneath a pile of bedding. Holding her sides, Fanny laughed wildly, defying him, proud of her exploit.

All at once a strange feeling came over Mr. Lewis. He became aware of the sun and of the charged spring atmosphere; he felt the ardor in Fanny's being. "Little brat," he said, and started after her. But she ran through the cabin, upsetting furniture, pushing chairs between herself and him, escaping him by rapid twists and turns. From basement to attic, shed to kitchen, among the overturned buckets and chairs, their chase continued. Finally, he caught up with her in a corner of her still littered room. She stood before him breathless, her arms open wide, her eyes brilliant, prepared for some incredible thing that she awaited without knowing what it was. At that moment, Mr. Lewis lost control of himself and with a violent gesture he threw her down on the bed.

V

The teacher spent a sleepless night. What had he done in that moment of passion? What treachery had he committed against this ignorant child? In what terrible danger had he placed her? And other, less noble fears lay heavy on his heart. He had compromised his personal honor, his future, the work to which he had dedicated himself, the respect that he received from everyone. It would all be destroyed if his mistake were ever known, if it should ever come to light through its fatal consequences. Feeling sorry for both himself and his companion, he searched desperately for a way out. But at every turn stood the specter of punishment and disaster.

He did not see her again until it was time for class, where he watched her with anxiety. Nothing in her manner betrayed the least concern; she looked up at him from her bench with the same soft, gay eyes. It reassured him a little. At least she did not hold it against him; or not yet, he added, as his sadness returned. He thought, also, of the pupils before him, who now regarded him so highly; how soon, perhaps, they would be witness to his disgrace, run after him with their taunts.

During the course of the day they found themselves alone for a moment. They felt differently towards each other now. But among the teacher's confused emotions were embarrassment and remorse; he stood before Fanny as though before a judge, not daring to look her in the face.

Finally, he said: "Fanny, I'm very upset. All along, I only wanted to help you; but now I'm afraid I've hurt you."

She gave him a perplexed look; then, with a little laugh, she said: "You certainly did hurt me! But we were fighting, weren't we? You gave me what I deserved for throwing the pillows. When I did it, I wanted something, I didn't know what. But I got it, Mr. Lewis, you gave it to me!"

She rushed into his arms, and her kisses had a new tenderness, an extraordinary emotion that astonished even her.

What could he do? She did not understand what had happened. He was distraught, adrift in a sea of grief and uncertainty. But from the depths of his distress rose up at last the one way left open to him, the bold decision that would keep them both from sinking.

"Fanny," he said, "you're very fond of me. What would you say to really marrying me and becoming my little wife? You know, to get married in the church and not to have to hide anymore when we want to have fun together?"

She was dumbfounded. To be Mr. Lewis' wife, to take his arm in the street, to walk with him to church, to buy his food and cook his meals, just like all the rest of the wives of the village with their husbands — it had never crossed her mind. Was it possible that he could have had such an idea? But when she considered the happiness that would be hers caring for her teacher, the idea seemed natural after all, completely within the order of things.

"You're not joking, Mr. Lewis? We would really be married? Of course I would like that — more than anything. Only, it's going to make the other girls awfully jealous. But it's our business, isn't it? If we want to get married, we'll get married, and that's that!''

"Yes, that's that, my little one. I think we should. I'll speak to Linda about it.''

Linda — the main obstacle. How would she ever accept such a strange idea? And for some time the teacher had noticed the many small attentions, the seductive looks given him which suggested some hidden purpose. A conflict between two rivals would certainly complicate matters. But it was a step that he had to take. When Linda returned home he went to her, feigning ease, and said: "Miss Linda, I'm thinking of doing something that I need your advice about. What would you think of my getting married?''

With visible interest, the young widow replied: "Why, dear Mr. Lewis, I think it would be a good thing for you to do. You must suffer from being alone; and it's high time you started raising a family.''

"That's precisely it. I'd hoped you'd approve. I'd thought — if it were possible — well, I'd thought of marrying your sister Fanny.''

"Fanny!'' said Linda with a start, feeling a cloud come over her.

"Yes. She's a wonderful child. I'm quite fond of her and I'd take good care of her.''

Flustered, Linda said again: "Fanny! But, dear Mr. Lewis, Fanny's not even fifteen years old; you're twice her age!''

"Granted. But physically she's no longer a child; she's almost as big as I am. And my age doesn't matter to her. She said she'd like very much to be Mrs. Lewis.''

"You've spoken to her, and she agrees? Mr. Lewis,

I'm amazed — the whole thing seems ridiculous to me." The surprise on her face turned to anger.

"Speak to her yourself, Linda. Fanny, come tell your good sister how much you want to be my wife."

Fanny, who had been waiting expectantly, appeared in the doorway of her room.

"Yes, Linda, it's fine with me. You've waited on me long enough. Mr. Lewis wants me to keep house for him. I know I can do it."

Linda felt trapped. She could not refuse to grant the wish of the man who had done so much for Fanny; she could not let him see how deeply disappointed she was. She did not for a moment suspect that the request had an ulterior motive.

"I can't figure it out," she said after a long silence, "how you could have had such an idea. It doesn't seem proper. But if the two of you are decided, there's nothing I can do to stop you."

VI

The news that Fanny was marrying the school-teacher caused great turmoil in the village. Everyone was disconcerted, and wondered how so serious and respectable a man could have fallen in love with a frivolous little girl, a tomboy fresh out of short dresses. On the playground the pupils whispered endlessly: "You know, Fanny, Fanny Johnston!"; and gossips prattled day after day: "Only yesterday she was climbing trees and tumbling with Charlie Ross!"

Linda was not the only one whose hopes were ended by the match. Other young women had pursued him, and one in particular called Martha Bledsoe, who thought she had made a conquest, complained widely and bitterly: ''Isn't it scandalous,'' she said, ''to see such a sensible man robbing the cradle? Couldn't he have found a woman his own age?''

But the gossip ended there. Mr. Lewis' reputation was so great and well-established that the harsh tongues hesitated at the threshold of more serious charges, and on the wedding day nothing showed of the village's disapproval. A curious crowd squeezed into the church; the choir to which Fanny belonged sang wedding songs; Linda and a cousin come from a plantation, escorted her through the decorated nave. In white muslin, her forehead wreathed in gardenias beneath a long pleated veil, Fanny, radiant with youth, managed her part without a fault. She was given to Mr. Lewis by the pastor. To all appearances, it was a marriage like any other.

They went to live in a rented house, for Linda found excuses not to have them with her, and without delay Fanny began in earnest to be a housewife. She scrubbed and washed from morning to night, and polished and waxed the furniture, eager for everything to be in order and glittering when her husband returned from school. There was always a fine meal cooking on the stove, and an elaborate dessert for Mr. Lewis. She served him as a young slave would have done, taking him coffee in bed, shining his shoes, trimming his nails, parting his hair in a perfect line; she paid attention to the least loose button and invisible tear. Such devotion was a joy for her and told of her pride in her duties as a wife. A single caress from the teacher made up for all her tiredness,

29

and the house resounded with happy songs: "Grandfather's Clock" was like a hymn to the happy moments of time. Peals of happy laughter would ring freely through the rooms. Although from a distance, Mr. Lewis took pleasure in this gaiety and youth; he accepted the riches of her generous heart, and congratulated himself for having done his duty.

But there was still a barrier between them: the insurmountable difference not so much in age as in their past relationship. The teacher, as though unable to help himself, still saw Fanny on a school bench. He could not think of her as fully his equal; she was the young pupil who had recited her lessons to him, and unconsciously, the patronizing instructor lived on within the husband. As for Fanny, the fact that her teacher was now her husband did not alter her manner towards him. She continued obstinately, even in intimacy, to call him "Mr. Lewis," respect restraining her loving passion, and only rarely, impelled by forces too long contained, did she give herself up to that openness of heart, those free and easy familiarities, which appealed to her vivacious nature. But their contrasting attitudes did not mar their peaceful accord or the love, unconventional as it was, that they had sworn for each other.

It was not long before they had visitors in great number who, under the pretext of congratulating them, took occasion to examine the furniture, their bedroom, and the way that Fanny kept house. Fanny's former girlfriends from school all found reasons for knocking on her door, and, casting envious glances at the curtains and ornate dishes which testified to her well-being, they exclaimed among themselves. Martha Bledsoe was among the first to offer her best wishes. Though older than Fanny, she knew her

30

well and had even used her at times to carry parcels to the schoolteacher. So it was with warm, cordial tones that she expressed her happiness at seeing Fanny married and her desire to be her friend, and to be of service if ever she were needed. "Mr. Lewis," she said, "could not have chosen a better mate." She was sure, she added, that theirs would be a simply ideal household.

Fanny was proud of these friendly visits and she responded to them with warm naiveté. She and her husband were invited to village meetings and to church-benefit nights. Everywhere her youth and her cascading laughter communicated joy and gaiety. But instinctively she maintained the decorum proper to her new position and the most malevolent tongues lacked gossip.

The birth of a child after a few months seemed the most natural thing in the world. It was a boy, light-skinned, whose vigor showed first of all in the volume of the cries with which he filled the house. From then on, the child-mother had a new reason for loving and giving herself. Between Mr. Lewis and the new Edward she learned the hardship of work and of nights without rest. She gave every tender care, every expression of love possible to the chubby infant who, little by little, was growing and awakening to the world, recognizing her and smiling at her. She no longer went out, not daring to leave him for an instant. "Grandfather's Clock" now had but one function, that of putting the baby to sleep. The evenings saw joys without end in which the father duly took part.

Then, three years in succession, she presented three more boys to Mr. Lewis. Unfortunately, the last one almost caused her death. She was taken hurriedly to the hospital where she remained for three months. Then, weakened after an operation which made it impossible for her to have more children, she returned home. But outwardly nothing appeared of the sickness inside which was eating away at her. Her face and figure kept their youthful grace, her limbs their suppleness, her manners their indestructible gaiety. She had just turned nineteen.

During her long absence, Martha Bledsoe had offered to look after the family. Installed in the house that she had dreamed of for herself, she demonstrated her capabilities as mistress of it. The children had all the care one could have wished. Mr. Lewis saw himself bathed in an atmosphere of leisurely comfort and discrete friendship which accorded with his tranquil nature. From time to time he would compare her sedate habits with the turbulent eagerness and taut nerves of his young wife — this period of calm seemed almost a respite. When Fanny returned they welcomed her happily; but, seeing the house organized with so much order and all functioning without a hitch like a silent machine, she had for a moment the feeling of being superfluous and of disturbing something.

She went back to her daily tasks, submerging herself in them entirely. Her life became nothing more than one job after another without cease, and all that sustained her was her love for her children and her desire to please Mr. Lewis. When the boys were old enough to go to school she took it upon herself to help them with their lessons, studying geography and grammar to be able to help them with these subjects. Thanks to her, the teacher's best pupils were in his own family.

VII

On the surface, their life went on unchanged as the days drifted by. But Mr. Lewis was no longer quite the same; a breach seemed to have opened in his feelings for Fanny and to be slowly widening with time. Perhaps, as time passed, the difference in their ages and personalities became more apparent; perhaps the mature man was tiring of the child who had never grown up. The care — assiduous as ever — that his young wife took of him left him indifferent now and sometimes made him impatient. Was there a deeper reason for this strange coldness? Concealing the suffering it caused her, Fanny sought to blind herself to it.

One day, on the road to the market where she bought their food, she met Charlie Ross. He was full-grown now, a large, strong, robust man with a sympathetic look about him, but whose reputation was hardly better than in the wild days of his childhood. His taste for adventure made his life unstable and prevented him from keeping a job, and his hot headedness often ran him afoul of the law. To the villagers he was a misfit who had to be tolerated as one of the family and upon whom they took pity. They had talked for a long time of how drunk he had been the day of Fanny's marriage. Ever since, when he met her he would endeavor to speak to her and renew their old friendship; but in return he got only a distant greeting or brief word; so this time he stood in front of her and blocked her way.

"Well! How's my friend Fanny?" he asked.

"You can see for yourself, Charlie, I'm alive."

"And your family? All healthy?"

"Yes, very, thank the Lord."

"Your husband's always busy, I imagine?"

"Mr. Lewis works a lot."

"Hm! He works all right. Tell me, are you sure you always know what he's working at?"

"No. But I suppose you do?"

"You said it; I know more than you think. Listen, it makes me sad to see a girl like you cheated on by an old man who should get down on his knees in front of you."

"You're as impertinent as ever, Charlie Ross."

"Impertinent? I've got eyes to see, and don't I run into your dear Mr. Lewis every Thursday strolling near the woods with a woman who's not you?"

"Please don't tell such lies!"

"I've never spoken a truer word. Ask Martha Bledsoe if I'm lying."

"I don't want to hear another word, Charlie Ross; you're an evil person."

"You ought to thank me instead of insulting me. And if you had any sense you'd treat Mr. Lewis the way he treats you. You'd find yourself a friend, somebody your own age."

He did not continue, for Fanny brushed him aside and went on towards the village, with her head held high.

But she knew that Charlie Ross had not lied. The mystery of Mr. Lewis' indifference was now cleared up. Someone else had taken her place, a supposed friend in whom she had foolishly put her confidence. Her honest soul was enraged at the thought. Her first instinct was to expose the vile treachery, to go find Martha Bledsoe and to tell her to her face what she thought of her. But that would mean humiliating Mr. Lewis also, and showing him the horror of what he was doing. How could she risk such action? A confrontation would destroy their peaceful existence, and what a shock it would be for her dear children who believed their parents to be so happy together. She felt alone and caught between love and propriety.

At home she said nothing of what she had learned. She gave her husband the same smiling reception. She wanted to think, to be very sure of what she should do.

Then, slowly, her great love got the better of her. To reveal her inner sorrow would make those whom she cherished unhappy, and extinguish forever any feeling that her unfaithful husband might still have for her. And, after all, who was she to go against Mr. Lewis; if he did not love only her, it was because she was unworthy of him. He shared a part of his heart with her, he provided a home for her, he was good to the children she had given him — and she still had her mission to serve him and to treat him with kindness.

A feeling of calm came over her and, at the same time, a desire for sacrifice. She would choose silence and tolerance; Mr. Lewis would know nothing of her secret anguish, and her beloved sons would console her for the pain their father inflicted on her.

VIII

A secret life began for Fanny, one of constant effort to hide her thoughts and to conceal with pretended gaiety what was really in her heart. On Thursdays her distress was heightened, for she knew now at what hour of the afternoon Mr. Lewis met Martha Bledsoe and she would imagine them walking hand in hand under the arch of the large elms. When her husband returned she would notice his cheerful manner and the sparkle in his eye, but it hurt her even more to think that he was false to her, that he so lowered himself to hide things from her. If only he would tell her everything, she would find the courage to face it. Further, the secret meetings were dangerous. Suppose others besides Charlie Ross noticed — tongues would be unleashed and shame brought upon the whole family. Thursdays became days of obsessive worry.

Thus, silence was not enough, only a heroic act could ease the situation; a sacrifice was called for. Her life's aim was to please Mr. Lewis; she would be able to show him how far she was willing to go to do just that, and she would save him from his own imprudence.

Following one of those days of torment, she went and sat beside him and said affectionately: "Mr. Lewis, would you grant me a favor?"

"Of course, Fanny, if I can."

"I feel tired, Mr. Lewis. Taking care of the house

and the children is exhausting. You know that I'm not the same as I was before. I think I need some rest."

"I understand, Fanny. Do you want me to send you to my sister's in Norfolk for a month? You'd be near the ocean and you wouldn't have to lift a finger."

"No, I don't want to go away for so long. But, could I, every week, have a day for myself to spend at Linda's?"

"That seems reasonable. One day a week, you say?"

"Yes, if I could. Thursday, for example. I could leave after lunch and come back the next morning. Since there has to be somebody here for you and the children, I'd thought that Martha Bledsoe . . ."

At the sound of the name, Mr. Lewis, faintly disturbed, turned to look at her. Was there a trap behind this request, he wondered? But he saw Fanny smiling, and the shadow across her face could have been from fatigue.

"Yes," he said coldly, "I suppose Martha Bledsoe would help us."

"Then it's agreed. Everything will take care of itself, you'll see, and you'll have everything you need."

"Everything takes care of itself," the schoolteacher repeated silently. However, he felt a certain sadness when two warm arms wound themselves around his neck and a soft, delicate voice whispered: "Thank you, my dear Mr. Lewis."

When Thursday arrived, Fanny, as though expecting its real mistress, put the house in perfect order. She changed the bedroom curtains, put clean sheets and an intricately embroidered colored spread on the bed, and she brought two bouquets of sweet peas from the garden and placed them in vases on the mantelpiece, taking a cruel joy in making things pleasant and agreeable for Mr. Lewis' adventure. If he was not happy, then he was difficult to please.

With a light bag in her hand she left the house and started down the village's main street. Like a homeless beggar in search of a refuge, she headed for the cabin where she had spent her childhood. She kept her composure before those whom she met and exchanged the usual greetings and pleasantries. But once at Linda's she gave way to tears, the first since her school days, and she cried for a long time on her sister's shoulder.

IX

The new arrangement was satisfying to all three of them for the time being. It gave Mr. Lewis the illusion of being able to move freely between the affections of the two women, and saved him the worry of secret meetings. Martha Bledsoe became aware of her greater power — she had forced her rival into her first retreat. Fanny, in her optimism, believed she had won her husband's gratitude. Her Thursdays in exile became almost routine, but the thought of her children prevented her from being fully resigned. Their care was now partly in the hands of Martha Bledsoe, but despite the woman's efforts, the children did not like her; they complained to their mother of her visits, only half understanding why she came.

38

Then an incident occurred which almost destroyed the peaceful framework which Fanny herself had created. One Friday, when she returned home, she found her husband sternly scolding their youngest boy, who had, it seemed, been disrespectful to Martha Bledsoe.

"I insist," the father said, "that you go to her and excuse yourself."

"I won't. I don't like that old maid," said the child.

"You won't? We'll see about that!"

Mr. Lewis moved towards the boy menacingly, determined that such insolence should be punished. But Fanny could stand anything except to see one of her children punished for Martha Bledsoe's sake.

"If you please, Mr. Lewis," she said, "don't touch the child. He won't do it again."

"This boy deserves a spanking," the teacher replied hotly. "I intend to see that he gets it."

"No, not for what he did; don't beat him for that."

Fanny stood erect, resolute; the tone of her voice was no longer that of a plea.

Mr. Lewis looked at her, surprised by his wife's open resistance, the first she had ever shown.

"I'm not used to asking permission in matters of raising my family," he said.

His hand up, he continued towards the child. But Fanny, beside herself, took hold of a chair that was within reach and lifted it over her shoulders. "Mr. Lewis," she said, "I swear to you upon my soul that if you touch him I'm going to strike you with this chair."

All four children stared in amazement. "Father," cried the oldest, "you're not going to fight with mama, are you?"

Mr. Lewis stopped. The whole family was against him. He did not dare risk a humiliating struggle by continuing.

"That's the way to make delinquents of your boys," he said angrily. Then he turned on his heels, swallowing his profound humiliation. Miss Bledsoe's honor went unavenged.

X

Despite this incident the days followed their normal course. The boy who had spoken out against his father was now seventeen. During the years, his father had seen to it that he continued his studies outside of school; he showed great capacity for learning, and Mr. Lewis was preparing him for Tuskegee Institute, dreaming of his son one day replacing him at the school. Edward Jr. enjoyed studying, but lacked order and tended to daydream. His was a poet's temperament; he was indifferent to the methodical investigation of questions whose answers he could often divine, and was enamored of brilliant ideas and impractical theorizing. His upright heart and spontaneous warmth were those of the mother whom he adored, and Fanny, proud of the boy, carried a secret preference for him.

Each of the other boys had his distinctive traits. George favored athletics and the active life; Frank had mechanical aptitudes and took pleasure in tools and scrap metal. The youngest, Robert, was the least serious of all. Nothing could hold the interest of this fickle nature, study less than anything else. Attracted by the woods and forbidden fishing ponds, ever involved in disputes and fist fights, he was the errant child Fanny had been, only rougher and more persistent.

Amidst his growing family, Mr. Lewis had aged; his teaching duties were becoming too much for him. He was no longer strong enough to control a group of rowdy youngsters and longed for less strenuous work. Because of his years of flawless service, he was able to obtain the job of village postmaster, and since there was little mail in such an isolated, backward place, the position was practically a sinecure. The salary was low and his family was forced to make unaccustomed sacrifices in food, clothing and coal.

Fanny took upon herself the greatest part of the privation, making sure that Mr. Lewis and the children were cared for first before she shared what little they had; she stayed awake late mending their shabby clothes which were ready for the rag-pile. Through her selfless economy and a partial scholarship from the state, Edward was able to leave in the autumn for college in Tuskegee. But his room and board involved many unforeseen expenses. Fanny decided to find a way to supplement their income, and went to work by the day as her sister Linda had done.

The Thursdays which should have allowed her some rest were now days of tiring labor, and she would have liked to have seen the last of Martha Bledsoe. But her rival's visits had become a fixed part of their lives, and it seemed too late to protest against them.

Several months went by and then misfortune fell even heavier upon the Lewis family. One night Fanny was hastily summoned, her husband had collapsed in his office. When she arrived he had just regained consciousness and it was evident from his inert body that he had suffered a paralytic stroke. Good care saved him, but he was left deprived of the use of his legs and was confined to a couch, dependent upon others to make the slightest move. He had to resign his job, cutting his family off from their sole means of subsistence other than the little Fanny earned. She now worked even more days than before and her evenings were spent doing the dishes and laundry that piled up in her absence. She was brave in spite of it all, and forced herself to continue to sing and laugh while hiding her exhaustion and fighting against worry. She was concerned especially for her sons' future. Edward Jr. was forced to leave school, to the regret of them all. Now back at home, he did his best to be of help, but, impractical as he was, met with little success. Anyway, he said, he was looking beyond his surroundings to the North where the black race was not held in such miserable subjection, where there was a future for every sincere effort. He was sure that he could put his talents to good use for the family whose protector he intended to be. He told his mother of his project, and poor Fanny, won over by his vision and refusing to show her grief at this new separation, used her last bit of money to outfit him and to buy him a ticket to Boston.

The first letters they received from him were encouraging. So far, it was true, he had found only a trifling job, but he had been promised a place as a reporter on a newspaper which was just starting and he had plans to teach literary history in the evenings to ambitious students. He even dreamed of starting a review where their essays could appear and where ideas and methods for the advancement of the black race could be exchanged. As soon as these enterprises were on the way, he would be assured an income sufficiently large for him to send them money regularly. In the meantime, he was happy to live in a place where the sons of Africa were treated like human beings. He was astonished to see blacks allowed on the same streetcars, in the same hotels, in the same theaters as whites. He had been in department stores where black women ran the elevators, and had seen black policemen directing traffic in the congested streets. The *Transcript*, Boston's most distinguished newspaper, had a black man as its literary critic and the best of Puritan society came to applaud the wonderful art of Roland Hayes. He found a great difference from the narrow-minded and contemptuous South where black persons were made to feel that they were still slaves, and which excluded them from its parks and even its sidewalks. This portrait was convincing to his family and gave them the patience to wait for the help that had not yet come.

The two other boys, Frank and George, found work here and there, though not without difficulty — part-time jobs which did little to ease their family's distress. They did not like to be an extra burden on their mother and father, the one overworked, the other infirm; and they, too, were persuaded that the North held their future. Soon they left, each with his small suitcase, to join their older brother.

Left behind alone, with no one to watch over him constantly, Robert was away from his family more often, apparently undisturbed by the problems at home. Then one day, before going out, he surprised his mother with a tender embrace; and that evening he did not come back. They looked everywhere for him, and notified the police in nearby towns. They heard nothing for two weeks and then a letter arrived. He had known, he said, the sacrifices that he was imposing upon them and so, in order to spare them, he had decided "to hit the road." He was in Charleston but was leaving that same day for the West. It was useless to search for him and they should not worry about him, he continued; he was fine, and had enough to eat, thanks to a little money he made working at odd jobs for some kind old ladies. He had no trouble hitchhiking. He would write later, giving them an address where they could send him news.

Fanny cried bitterly when she read the letter. Her son, then, was a tramp, a vagabond who traveled the highways, always in search of a meal and a place to rest, riding freight cars, fighting rain and snow, sleeping under the stars or in barns or sheds. Her heart sank at the thought.

XI

Now that her children were gone she was left alone with her crippled husband, the Mr. Lewis whom she still worshipped but who treated her with indifference, and took her kindnesses as though they were his due. For in his helpless state he had grown sullen; he spent his time daydreaming or reading, answering her in monosyllables. He had acquired that egoism of many ill persons who demand the world's attention and then complain of imaginary neglect.

Fanny got little sympathy from the villagers during these sucessive trials; they held her responsible for her misfortune, it was her punishment, they believed, for having seduced Mr. Lewis into a foolish marriage. Charlie Ross alone offered to help. He came without being asked to relieve her of any heavy labor; he raked the garden, cut wood, replaced fallen boards and took Mr. Lewis out in his wheelchair. But he also blamed Fanny. When they were alone, he would say: "You see what you got by marrying your old schoolteacher." Another time he reminded her: "You owe me two kisses that you've never paid me; why not pay me now?" But Fanny replied: "No, Charlie, I can't do that; you know I'm a married woman."

More and more she felt weary and worn. Now in her early thirties, her whole life had been one of work and service to others. It was as if a blindly spinning wheel had caught her and held her fast. Time had stopped; through all the years of devoted service and naive submission to her teacher she had remained a child. Her very sons had passed through her arms like living dolls. But now her childhood had abruptly ended; the young woman she could have been, who had always been there in her lively eyes, her silver voice, her fresh, genial nature, had awakened as from a dream to find that she had not yet lived. Fanny was terrified of a future which promised only hard, thankless duties. She remained faithful to Mr. Lewis — her life was his to use — but her love, treated so contemptuously, had lost its passion and was now little more than affectionate pity.

Martha Bledsoe still stood between them. She prided herself upon her attention to Mr. Lewis and enjoyed playing the role of devoted nurse. "Fanny," she would say, "is nothing but a big child; she doesn't know a thing about caring for the sick. The poor man is lucky to have someone who can give him the care he needs at least once a week."

In her solitude Fanny thought often of her sons. They were the last refuge for her forlorn heart. At night she would dream of them fighting fantastic creatures or struggling against torrents. The news she received from them explained her disquiet. The two who had left to join their brother in Boston had not found what they expected. Work was scarce and never lasted long, they complained, and their ambitions had met with one obstacle after another. The North was far from being the paradise for the black race that they had thought. The friendliness that they had spoken of was often little more than a mask which hid a crueler kind of ostracism. Exept in the rarest instance, only the lowest jobs were available to them, and at a slave's wage. They barely survived off the pittance they earned cleaning yards, unloading trucks and repairing streets; and they lived together in a single, small room where they cooked and did their laundry. They felt lost without their mother. Each week they pooled their money, and by finding ways to live even more cheaply, they were able to send a little money home. Reluctantly, Fanny took their kind offering.

Edward, however, had not given up hope. While awaiting his job with the newspaper, he worked addressing advertising circulars for a cure-all remedy. The agency provided him with a desk in the hall at which to work. He took advantage of the situation to further his own projects, laboring into the night writing advertisements for his lessons and requests for subscriptions to his review. The magazine's prospectus was already drawn up and the first number was ready for the printer. Mr. Lewis had taken an interest in it and waited daily for its arrival, but all that came to allay his impatience were circulars wrapped in pink paper announcing the cure-all.

From Robert, the wanderer, they received a postcard from time to time, always with the same message: he was still traveling across the country; he found many companions along the way, and had seen camps full of men from all over. They helped each other, he said, by marking hospitable houses with chalk and exchanging food and tobacco. He had become hardened to the sun and fatigue and paid no heed to tomorrow. Perhaps, after all, he was the happiest, Fanny thought. But each stage of his journey took him farther from his home and seemed to her to be one more step towards their complete separation.

She was sure that her three other sons would fare better with her guidance and she thought constantly of being with them. If she were to work alongside them, together they could support Mr. Lewis and make his life more comfortable. Her husband would have nothing to regret; Martha Bledsoe could come to live with him — was she not his real friend? Besides, his condition had improved; he could now get up by himself and was able to take a few steps with the help of a walking stick. The nurse's job had eased somewhat. Fanny would go to the big city where her sons were struggling and devote herself to them as well as to their father; it was the only way for her to do her duty.

But how could she leave the man who was so close to her heart, who might, perhaps, still need her without knowing it? The problem was anguishing. Each morning she was ready to resolve it, but each night she was as timid and as unsure as ever.

She mentioned her plan first to Linda. The stern widow disapproved immediately. "The Lord sends you misery for you to carry it together," she said, "not for you to avoid it by separating. You think you have your husband's and your children's interests at heart, but be careful that it's not because you're tired of your duties and want a change so you can be freer. The devil has many ways to draw us into his traps."

Fanny said no more; she herself did not know the real reason for the way she felt.

XII

But she finally made her decision, arriving in Boston still upset by what she had gone through. Her departure had not caused as much disturbance as she had feared. Mr. Lewis was surprised at first, but he quickly realized the advantages that the plan held for him, and in his cold acquiescence Fanny could see how distant her husband had become.

She went to see each of the families for whom she had worked and each kindly gave her money for her trip, and, together, a month's food for Mr. Lewis. Martha Bledsoe agreed to live at the house, attracted by the hope of an easy life where her needs would be looked after. Charlie Ross looked sad to see Fanny leave, but he said: "You're doing the right thing. Maybe you'll see me do the same, one of these days." Linda, however, remained unreconciled; she continued to suspect that Satan lay somewhere at the bottom of it all.

Her sons, happy to have their mother with them at last, gave her a joyful reception. They had reserved a room for her in their boarding house but only until a home was found in which they could again live as a family. She started right in washing, putting things in order and cooking the meals, assuming an old yoke with a new, jubilant heart.

She rediscovered her laughter and all her songs and wit. It was as if a heavy burden had fallen from her shoulders; she felt light and free, as young as the young men around her. She was seeing the big city for the first time and it fascinated and excited her: the enormous buildings with their endless storeys, the streets lined with splendid shops, overrun with streetcars and automobiles and teeming with busy crowds, filled her with the same wonder as had, in another time, the fields of Greenway with their profusion of flowers and birds. She loved to walk aimlessly seeking new and unusual things. Instincts dormant since her childhood were reawakening; she felt within her the adventuresome, impetuous life of old.

She had not forgotten her mission, however, and had already begun her plan of attack by sending her sons out in search of the elusive "job," making sure that they overlooked no possibility. Soon, Frank found work in a garage where his mechanical abilities served him well. George, while waiting for something better, delivered groceries. Edward, instead of merely sending the circulars extolling Remedy-X, was now writing them, and thus made more money. But, worth more to them than their jobs was Fanny's confidence and good humor. It made their life together warm and happy. Every day she thought of Mr. Lewis, and wrote to him often. She deprived herself to add to the amount of money that she could send him. But she did not regret the separation. Life in the new land held her in its grip.

XIII

Roxbury is the Harlem of Boston, a vast and ancient suburb where the African race, having gradually replaced the original inhabitants, feels at home. Within it are more than thirty thousand men and women, black, half-black, and every shade of brown, who carry on a valiant struggle against the economic and other forces which threaten to crush them. They come from every part of the Union, every corner of America. Natives of the South know each other by their lyrical inflexions and long vowels; those from Chicago speak with the accent of the Great Lakes; while those born there speak Yankee, or something like it. Some have come from Bermuda, Cuba, Jamaica, Santo Domingo; largely uneducated West Indians who still carry traces of superstition and voodooism. Others have emigrated from the Cape Verde Islands, putting between themselves and their tiny hamlets the whole breadth of the Atlantic. There are the Portuguese, a primitive tribe, but energetic and resourceful. These diverse origins form as many separate groups. The West Indian remains a stranger to the American, and both speak of the Portuguese with disdain; and among Americans, the Southerner has little to do with the Northerner. Stranger still are the social distinctions based upon the different shades of skin. Light-and dark-skinned persons feel uncomfortable together, and an olive-complexioned girl is thought to lower herself by marrying a boy with ebony- or even mahogany-colored skin. Similarly, those with straight hair look down on those with kinky hair. These distinctions persist in spite of the fact that members of the different groups are forced to live side by side and that there are often individual ties between them.

The people are poor but not wretched, for they have admirable resources in their ingenuity, their frugality, their gaiety and endurance. Their dwellings are small and scanty, but their cleanliness conceals their poverty; one rarely finds a slum. Meals, of necessity, are simple, but their nourishment is apparent in the plump, well-developed women and children. The children, far from being ragamuffins, always go to school in clean clothes, and the boys' hair is shaved close to their heads while the girls wear carefully plaited pigtails. At church on Sundays, their parents shine with a middle-class elegance.

But it takes a lot of forethought and ingenuity to maintain this standard of living. While the husband works slavishly at a menial job, the wife washes floors in a hotel or does cleaning in rich people's houses. The children run errands and shine shoes and gather firewood for the winter from refuse piles. But help is always given to those who need it. A family with two rooms who, in fact, need four, finds a way to put up those out of work or with no place to stay. This mutual assistance is considered a duty which everyone accepts and benefits from in turn. Even one of its less modest forms, the common-law marriage, is looked upon with great tolerance. The young woman or the widow with no means of support, or the abandoned wife, is readily adopted by "friends;" or if the woman is working, she takes in a "friend." The institution of the "boyfriend" reigns throughout Roxbury; it is so common as to be respectable, an easier, more convenient kind of marriage. A woman says "my boyfriend" as simply as she would say "my husband," and the two are as faithful to each other as conventionally-married couples.

Of course there is an underworld in Roxbury made up, as everywhere, of fools, parasites and miscreants of all sorts, none of whom is any better or worse than those found in white communities.

Hard-working and poor, Roxbury is happy, nonetheless. There is more laughter there than in well-off Back Bay, and, as hard as life can be for its people, the dances and the frequent parties are evidence of the pleasure they take in life. Sadness comes only with the thought of the heavy burden they bear because of their dark skins. In Roxbury's music is found the warmth and variety of its soul: irrepressible jazz with its rousing challenge, spirituals full of mystical confidence, and the blues with their melancholy wail and lamentations of servitude.

Roxbury is a crowded anthill fraught with singular, colorful life. One witnesses there the struggle of a downtrodden race to find its place in the sun, a foreign sun not of its own choosing. One is surrounded by humble scenes at all levels of the human drama — success, trials, defeat, humor, tragedy; but there perhaps more than anywhere else, courage and infinite patience go hand in hand.

Roxbury, then, like Harlem, is a flower from the hothouse of Africa, which, though unaccustomed to the hostile winter, and still weakened from its violent transplantation, has taken root, growing and spreading out in search of walls and columns to which to attach itself. The difficult and disquieting problem caused by the continuous expansion of the black race is white America's punishment for an ancient crime against black humanity.

XIV

As soon as they were able to pay the rent, Fanny and her sons moved into the second story of a building on Shawmut Avenue at the heart of Roxbury. They occupied six rooms, one of which was for the boarder they hoped to have. Their apartment overlooked a narrow courtyard crossed by clothes-lines and crowded with overflowing garbage cans where the surrounding twelve families hung their washing. Flanked on both sides by identical dwellings, the building, except for the forty-five minutes of each day when the sun shone directly upon it, lay in dim, hazy light that came through shaft-like spaces at either end. At the rear there was a steep staircase which led to the ground. The landings were cluttered with pieces of metal, empty boxes and broken chairs, through which cats of every color crept stealthily, some mild, others menacing. Electric wires could be seen all over, but inside the building only gas lamps could be found; and the plumbing, often the pride of modern houses, was still primitive here. It was a building that had once housed people of means but which, through years of neglect, had become obsolete and dilapidated.

Fanny had chosen it, nevertheless, after a careful

search. She was satisfied and felt at ease; each of her sons had his own bed, and a table and trunk for himself between four papered walls. In the kitchen there were new utensils and a nickel-plated stove. Water flowed freely from the pipes at a simple turn of the tap. It was luxury when compared to the cabin in Greenway, even if the latter had had sunshine.

Wanting to know her neighbors, Fanny went from landing to landing introducing herself and spreading her contagious laughter, graciously offering her services. They all found her friendly and pleasant. Then she invited them to a party to celebrate her new apartment. They could get to know each other and play whist, and her son George would play the accordion for those who wanted to dance. Also, she asked them to contribute food for the meal at the end of the evening.

When Saturday night arrived, there was a lot of activity on the Lewis' floor. Up the stairs came gay and talkative company. Mrs. Sidney, a widow who lived below, was the first to arrive, accompanied by two young women who roomed with her. Then Tommy Rollins, a respected man who drove a truck for a wholesale house, came with his wife. The tune of a popular song and the sound of dancing on the stairs announced Joe Bradshaw, a cheerful, easy-going man who worked at the same garage as Frank. Maude Olliver, a tiny, tranquil, well-dressed woman came down from the third floor where she lived with her sister. Her husband had left her and, too indifferent towards men to find someone to support her, she took in laundry when she could. Two other guests, Mr. and Mrs. Lattimore, had left their five smaller children with the eldest and were happy to have the evening to themselves after a hard day. George had taken an interest in a pretty girl named Lizzie Carter, who was a customer at the grocery store where he worked, and she had come as his guest.

Enough players were found for five tables of whist. The games were lively and trinkets made out of *papier mâché* served as prizes for the winners. But after an hour the young people called for music and soon the floor shook beneath the fast rhythm of the dancers. After several two-steps, the couples danced them-selves into a frenzy to the faster beats of the Char-leston and the Black-bottom as the onlookers shouted and clapped their support. During the intermissions Joe Bradshaw tap-danced, his heels clacking rapidly like a machine-gun. Also, two women sang the blues, lamenting betrayed love with sobbing notes and cries of savage despair.

Suddenly, someone asked: "Where is Irene? Irene didn't come?" They looked around, repeating: "Where is Irene?"

"The woman who lives on the third floor, to the left?" asked Fanny. "I'm sure I invited her, and she was counting on being with us."

"You never know with Irene," said Maude Olli-ver, smiling. "But, what if we go and get her?"

"That's the thing to do," several people said, and started towards the stairs. "Let's call her. Hey, Irene!"

"You all know she's deaf," said Mrs. Lattimore. "Two or three of you ought to go and bring her here. But, maybe," she added, "she's not in a mood for dancing. She had a fight with her boyfriend."

A group of them went upstairs and reappeared soon with triumphant shouts, practically carrying Irene.

Irene was a woman of uncertain age and singular appearance. She was bronze-colored with a strong, muscular build and a short, flat face. She had a way of staring at others that seemed odd until one realized that there was a glass eye where a real one should have been. She was an energetic person, free and straightforward: a character, who was known in the quarter for her loud gaiety and violent anger. "She's a good girl," people said, "but don't cross her." When she lost control of herself she would use anything in reach, cups, casseroles and even knives. But she was the life of every party. She entered waving her hands in greeting.

"Why didn't you come?" the others cried.

"I have company," she said. "But Lawrence can wait: he's had one too many and he's sound asleep."

"I'll bet he's sleeping," Mrs. Rollins whispered in her husband's ear. "She hit him over the head with her broom."

They began to dance again and Irene moved faster and laughed louder than all the rest.

At midnight everybody was ready to eat. The guests went into the kitchen where the tables from the other rooms had been placed together and unpacked the food they had brought. There were ham sandwiches, fried-egg sandwiches, smoked sausages, potato salad, banana fritters, and Southern-style corn pone. Maude, who had lived among the Portuguese, had brought a plate of *jacasida*, their favorite recipe, made from kidney beans and steamed rice. They put it all together and then served themselves. Fanny furnished tea and cakes. At this point the conversation became more personal. They told each other the latest news and described recent misfortunes. George spoke softly to Lizzie Carter, and the other boys stood next to Mrs. Sidney's boarders. Mrs. Sidney herself cornered Fanny and told her that she wanted very much to get to know her. She invited her warmly to come to see her. "We give parties, too," she said, "and I'm sure you would enjoy yourself. A woman all alone like you must get bored. You seem so young, and with your charming ways, you would make a lot of friends fast."

"I have more than I need," said Fanny, laughing and pointing to her three sons; "look at my three sweethearts." She promised to go down, though, and help her friend, who complained that her apartment was very large and that she had more work than she could cope with.

It was after one o'clock when the group broke up with noisy good-byes. The party had been a complete success. It had given Fanny a glimpse of life in the big city and she was excited by what she had seen.

XV

Edward too, whom misfortune had pursued so long, seemed to have turned the corner. "Mama," he said one evening, "I've got a surprise for you. A little while ago I took a civil service test for a place in the post office. Something made me want tō do the kind of work that my father had done. I didn't say anything to you because I was afraid of disappointing you, but, here — look at the results!"

He handed her a letter with an official heading. Smiling radiantly, Fanny read the announcement of her son's success. He was asked to report in eight days to the main office in Boston to begin work. He would begin by sorting mail; that was the first step towards the grade of postman and more important duties.

"It's wonderful, dear!" Fanny cried, wrapping her arms around his neck. "I always believed that one day you would be something."

"You understand, I'm not going to give up my other interests for this," Edward continued. "On the contrary. This job will let me get on faster. I'll have more money for both the magazine and my night courses. Sorting mail isn't very interesting, but the hours are short; I'll have some time to myself."

"I hope that in the future we'll be able to send a little more to Mr. Lewis," said Fanny coolly.

"Why, mama, don't be upset. In no time we'll all be a lot better off."

Edward began his new job on the appointed day. He had to replace the night workers at an early hour, so each morning Fanny rose before daylight to prepare his breakfast and lunch. His work was over by early afternoon and he gave all his spare time to the projects he dreamed of. He wrote articles and poetry for his magazine as well as appeals for suscribers, and solicited the aid of famous black writers. His correspondence grew, and it was with pride that Fanny brought him handfuls of letters from the mailbox. As much as she could she served as his secretary, helping him to sort things and to answer his mail so that he could get a few extra hours of sleep.

Around the same time Frank became the chauffeur of a rich Jewish merchant who traveled between his office in Boston and his home in Auburndale. Frequently he drove the man's wife into the city to shop, and on Sundays, if the weather was nice, he drove the whole family to the country. But outside of these duties he had a lot of free time. All that was asked of him during these hours was to run a few errands and to tend the lawn. Of all the groups that make up the American people, the Jews are freest from the prejudices of race and color. Suffering themselves from ostracism, they understand the unjust cruelty of it, and look almost fraternally upon its other victims.

Frank was obliging and polite, so his employer was soon pleased with him; and hearing him speak repeatedly of his mother and of how much he loved her, he allowed the boy, in his idle hours, to take her riding in the luxurious automobile. Fanny, child-like, was enchanted by the silk curtains, the plush cushions, the speed and the changing scenery. Once again she was the young girl of Greenway out seeking adventure; but instead of flying through the roads and the fields alone, a genie was carrying her far away on miraculous wings.

XVI

Fanny's neighbors were now her friends and often came to visit her. Maude Olliver came most frequently, and the two women had long chats together. Maude, who was taciturn and reserved, was hesitant to speak openly of herself at first, but, because of Fanny's frankness, she soon took her into her confidence and told of her life. Her mother had been a negress but through her father she was descended from an authentic Indian tribe known as the Masphee, who lived on the ancient hunting grounds of their ancestors near Cape Cod, and who were slowly disappearing. Her father had inherited the wandering spirit of his ancestors, and it was not long before he left his wife (or, as Maude said unhesitatingly, "the woman who was supposed to be his wife"). In despair, her mother put her in the hands of a woman who had the means to keep her. Of her childhood, spent under this woman's watchful but austere eye, she remembered most of all the strict supervision and the harsh punishment she got for the slightest misdeed. She was only fourteen when her guardian died, so her mother, who had married in the meantime and now had two other children, was forced to take her back.

Having been so long forgotten, Maude was a stranger in the family. Her mother gave her the toughest chores to do and denied all her requests. With unspoken contempt she blamed her own shame on her daughter, and even held it against her for having been born. Her half-sisters were hostile and condescending towards her, and her stepfather treated her brutally, without pretext. The only time she felt free of all of them, was at school, and on her way to and from it. From her playmates, she learned things that she had never known. Occasionally a boy from her class would walk with her, taking care to leave her before they came in view of the house for fear of what would happen if they were seen.

"One evening," she said, "I was sitting on the doorstep taking the summer air. I saw a young boy I didn't know. He came up to me and said: 'Hello. Are you bored?'

'That's none of your business,' I said, and gave him a hard look.

'Don't get angry,' he said. 'I see you so much when I come by here I feel like I know you.'

'Well,' I said, 'I don't know you.'

"Then he told me all about himself, that he didn't live far away and that he had a job in the gasworks. He ended by telling me that he liked the way I looked and that he wanted to be friends with me. You know how it is. He was good-looking and I fell for him. 'I'd like that,' I told him, 'but I'm forbidden to go out.' He whispered and said: 'We'll find a way to see each other,' and started to sit down beside me. But just then the window opened and my mother saw us. 'Maude!' she yelled — she was furious — 'What's going on?' You can imagine the lecture I got, and the beating, too. I was over sixteen but they beat me anyway."

"So it ended right there," Fanny said.

"Oh, no. He would watch for me after school and after church, too, and he left me notes in the cracks of telephone poles. Believe me if you will, Mrs. Lewis, after two months we were married."

"Married. Heavens, you were impatient youngsters."

"Married secretly. I knew that my mother would never allow it, so we went to a nearby town, lied about our ages, and in the time it takes to say it, we were married. That night I got home late. I couldn't help it. So they beat me and put me to bed. But during the night I got my clothes together and ran to meet him outside where he was waiting for me. He had a furnished room by the port where we stayed for three weeks."

"Three weeks? And after?" said Fanny anxiously.

"Were you sorry so soon?"

"Not at all. He was a good boy; he worked, he didn't drink. We were happy as angels. But my mother found out where I was. She sent the police. They wanted to arrest me for immoral conduct, but when I stuck my marriage license under their noses, they had no choice but to let me be. Then I was dragged to court and the marriage was annulled. I was a minor, and this and that. I cried, I bit them, but nothing worked. I had to go back with them. But, dear girl, I can't tell you everything at once. I hear my sister coming up the stairs; I've got to go warm up supper."

"And this sister?" asked Fanny.

"Oh, it's my half-sister. She's out of work and I've taken her in. She hasn't always been very nice to me, but you've got to forget, don't you?"

XVII

Fanny now wrote every week to Mr. Lewis. She sent him all the money she could put aside, gave him news of his sons, and assured him of her constant affection. He rarely answered. Martha Bledsoe wrote in his stead. Her letters were curt; she sent little news except to say that Mr. Lewis' condition was no better and that it was hard to give him all the attention he needed. She made it apparent that things were not perfect between them. From Linda, who was still angry about her sister's departure, and who, besides, could neither read nor write, there had been no word.

Thus, Fanny was surprised one day to receive a long letter written in her sister's name.

"Sister Fanny," the message began, "I have to inform you that your husband is no longer with Martha Bledsoe. She is a woman who always looks out for herself first, and she doesn't have it in her to put up with sacrifices. She thought she was doing something smart by taking Mr. Lewis away from you, but she soon saw that it meant nothing but hard work and slavery. Then, one morning, without a word to anybody, she left. The Lord only knows how long he would have stayed all alone if Charlie Ross hadn't stopped by. He didn't have a thing to eat and was in his chair, trembling. You understand the predicament the poor man was in. Seeing him so helpless, I offered to have him here with me, and he has been here for two weeks now. Don't go and think, Fanny, that I did it to please myself. It's a heavy load that I'm carrying. But you weren't there to take care of your husband and I felt obliged to do it for you. If you had listened to me and followed the path of righteousness, none of this worry would have come about. It's up to you now to see what you have to do and to do it. I can't say that Mr. Lewis asks for you. He doesn't speak of you, and he seems happy to have me to look after him. But you're the one who married him and you should accept the consequences. I want him to stay here with me. That's not the question. But my conscience obliges me to remind you of your duty. I hope that you are well. Linda."

Fanny was taken aback by the letter. She was bewildered. The pity she felt for Mr. Lewis, the anger she felt towards the unworthy Martha Bledsoe, the remorse caused by her sister's reproaches were met by concern for her sons. She was afraid to leave them;

they had a good life together. Her head in her hands, she tried for a long time to come to a decision, but her soul floundered in uncertainty.

That evening when the three boys were seated at the table she showed them the letter. "What should I do?" she asked. They were quick to reply. "Mama, you can't leave," they said together. "It's a good thing for father to be rid of Martha. He'll be better taken care of at your sister's — and the care he gets will be genuine, not hypocritical. Without you, we wouldn't know what to do. We would have to separate, we wouldn't have the same courage to face things, and then, since our expenses would be higher, father would suffer. Stay here, it's better for everybody."

Fanny listened to them thoughtfully. "I understand you," she said, "you know where my heart lies. I'll make a decision tonight."

She did not sleep at all that night. The problem seemed truly to be too much for her; she did not have the experience to deal with it. Her personality was simple; she could cope with straight roads without obstructions, with problems that still let her sing. Here all was tangled. She had to unravel the skein of duties before spinning their yarn, to know before acting; one was as hard as the other.

Her decision, taken at dawn, was like an act of blind will. While it was still early she went into Edward's room. She kissed him and said as she held back her tears, "Son, I have decided to leave for Greenway." Then, placing her hand over his mouth she continued, "Don't tell the others before tonight. While you all are at work, I'll leave and take the train for the South. I don't have the courage to say goodbye to them. It's already too much for me to speak to you. But we'll always be together. I won't stop thinking of you.''

XVIII

The next day a car thronged with a motley crowd carried Fanny towards the South. She cried and felt helpless as she watched her happy life slipping away and out of sight with every field and village that they passed. She had had a pleasant dream; now it had given way to a brutal awakening. She had thought to have escaped the bondage in which she had been held since her childhood as punishment for a moment of folly. Now she had to go back to it, to yield again to oppression. With every turn of the wheels, her peaceful days made beautiful by the presence of her sons, were pushed farther away. Linda and Mr. Lewis seemed to beckon her with cruel gestures. To her dismay she was aware of a bitter feeling of revolt; she almost hated them. During the first few hours she cried without stopping, sometimes in silence and sometimes biting her handkerchief to stifle the sound of her sobbing. Several persons turned to look at her, their curiosity aroused by such open sorrow. Finally, when her tears had stopped, Fanny, exhausted by the previous night, fell asleep in her seat.

When she awoke, the train had gone past Baltimore, and Washington was only a few miles away. There she would have to change trains and soon after she would be in the real South. She was distracted by having to get her bag and to erase the traces of her tears, but when she boarded the next train she was reminded abruptly of where she was; she had to go to a car that was for black people only.

Soon she began to recognize a change in the landscape. The countryside presented the more familiar scenes of old, the grass was dryer and less strong, the fields were already crested with white bolls of cotton for as far as the eye could see. Among the serried stalks, like large poppies, swayed the red bandanas of the pickers. Towns shrank to villages and villages to hamlets. Miserable cabins stood like markers along the neglected roads, cabins that held not only black people but a whole class of white farmers who subsisted on a mere fraction of what they grew — "white trash," whom even the Negroes despised. The bright sun shed its shimmering heat down upon the whole scene.

At the small stations blue-shirted workers and mothers with small, lightly-dressed children, got on and off the train. Their voices and laughter sounded to Fanny like an echo of her own. She, too, was a child of this land and she knew again the feelings that she had once had for it. She was calm now and together with the familiar scenes came memories which remained dear to her. She saw herself back at school or playing in fields as green as the ones before her. She thought more peacefully of Mr. Lewis. She had so truly, sincerely loved him. He, too, for a while had distinguished her with his affection. She thought again of their meetings after class, those secret excursions to the stream hidden in the woods, and their race through the cabin on that thrilling morning which had decided their fate. In spite of everything she had no regrets, for those days were the finest of her life. Poor Mr. Lewis was now crippled and sad. Pity for him kept her from feeling sorry for herself. She had been his servant and would be again. Once more, now that Martha Bledsoe was no longer between them, he would give his heart to her and that would make up for everything.

Thus reconciled, Fanny stepped down from the train at the Wildwood station and started on foot across the country towards Greenway. She had two miles to go over ground that she had traveled many times; it was as though she were following her own footprints. Tired when she reached the village limits, she sat for a while on a rock in the shadow of an oak to wipe the perspiration from her face, stopping also, perhaps, because of a last-minute hesitation before her sacrifice. Soon she rose and walked down the hamlet's only street. There were houses on both sides, but because of the heat at this hour, it was almost deserted. A few dogs strolled here and there, and on the porches of the houses half-naked babies were sleeping. Then she noticed a woman seated just in front of her door in the shade of a tall wistaria. It was Sandra Nicholson, an acquaintance from school who had married not long after she did. A look of stupefaction appeared on the woman's face when she saw Fanny, and then the beginning of a smile changed to a look of curiosity.

"Hello, sister Sandra," said Fanny, stopping. "Do you remember an old friend?"

"Well! I'll be hanged if it isn't Mr. Lewis' Fanny," said the woman, looking at her from head to foot.

"Herself. How are you? And how are things in Greenway?"

"Oh, like always; nothing new. But, my goodness, neither I nor anybody else was expecting to see you around here again."

"Really? And why not?" asked Fanny, somewhat

68

surprised.

"Well, that would take too long to explain," muttered her acquaintance. "We thought you had picked up and left for good."

"But you see I didn't," laughed Fanny. "You can't get rid of a bad penny so easily. I hope to see you soon."

Fanny went on. She was intrigued by this ambiguous attitude. What was the matter with Sandra? Some minutes later she reached her sister's door. Her heart was beating rapidly as she raised the metal hammer — it was the beginning of a new period in her life, but she struck hard upon the door. Moments later, Linda stood before her, looking as surprised as Sandra Nicholson had been.

"Is it you, Fanny?" Linda cried. She stood rigid in the doorway.

Moved, Fanny stepped forward to embrace her sister and said: "Well, yes. You wrote me, didn't you?"

"Of course," Linda replied, obviously embarrassed. "Of course. But I didn't..., we didn't ask you..., Well, come in and make yourself at home. Mr. Lewis is going to be very surprised."

"He's not any worse, is he?"

"No, he's much better. He's sitting out on the back porch because of the heat."

"You seem to be in good health. You don't have too many problems making ends meet?"

"The Lord helps me, Fanny. Do you want a cup of tea? Or do you want to see Mr. Lewis right away?"

"Yes, I would like to see Mr. Lewis."

"It would be better if I warn him first."

She disappeared, closing the bedroom door behind her. Fanny remained standing, still holding her valise in her hand. She was disturbed by the way her sister was acting — she was so cold, and there was so much ceremony.

After some time which seemed unnecessarily long, Linda returned and motioned for her to come. She followed her through the two rooms to the trellised porch where a soft breeze was blowing.

Mr. Lewis seemed to have changed very little; she noticed that he was seated in the same chair in which he had been sitting twelve months before. Her heart went out to him. This was the teacher she had revered and to whom, even from afar, she had dedicated every day of her life.

"Mr. Lewis!" she cried; then she rushed over to him and embraced him. But she drew back quickly, for her husband looked at her as if she were a stranger; his icy expression seemed to push her away.

"So, there you are, Fanny," he said after a while. "You're a little late, it seems to me; but I'm happy to see you anyway. How are the children? What's become of them up there? And you. Why did you come?"

"To see you, Mr. Lewis. I heard of what you had been through . . ."

"Oh, that. Well, you know, when your own family goes against you, you may as well expect others to do the same.

"Well," Fanny replied, ignoring his remark, "I've come to help you. I've come to see if you need me."

"I've done without you for a long time now, Fanny. I'm not badly off here, as you can see. Your sister is a conscientious person; she treats me like a friend."

This time she did not know what to say. "Then you don't want me to stay here with you?" she stammered.

70

"I did not say that. But is it really necessary? You should have waited until I called for you. Linda feels the same way. But we'll speak of it some more. Stay a few days, at least."

So this was the welcome she got, her compensation for what she had left behind. Among her muddled emotions was a terrible sadness at being rejected by the two people who, other than her sons, meant the most to her.

"Come put your things away," Linda said coldly.

They went into the next room. Then, unable to stand it any longer, Fanny threw herself down on a chair and shivered inwardly as though waking from a dream.

"Mr. Lewis doesn't love me anymore," she said.

At first, Linda did not reply and they remained silent with their thoughts. Finally, she spoke.

"My dear," she said, "everything that has happened is your own doing. I warned you of what your behavior would lead to; and now you're surprised at your punishment? Like everybody, Mr. Lewis is faithful to those who treat him right."

There was a note of triumph in Linda's words. More than divine justice, was this not simply a rival's revenge, taken after so many years?

Fanny realized the injustice of what her sister was saying. She had never stopped helping her husband. But she was too overcome to reply.

"But, regardless," Linda continued, "stay with us as long as you like. And if you and Mr. Lewis can't get together, you can always go back to your boys."

"Yes," Fanny thought, "my sons are waiting for me." They were a bright spot in the cloudy sky. But, she wondered, was there not some way she could satisfy both of her loves?

71

XIX

Her trip had served no purpose. She was an intruder. This would be no more than a simple visit, then; which, after all, was what they wanted. Today was Saturday. She would remain until Thursday for appearances' sake, and would try to be brave meanwhile, and to make the best of things.

That evening the three of them sat in the low-ceilinged kitchen as Fanny told of her life in the North. She told of her sons' jobs. Mr. Lewis was interested in Edward most of all. "He is picking up where I left off," he said. "I'm confident that he'll go far." With this subject they warmed slightly to each other, but soon the coolness returned. Not a word was said about the question that was foremost in their minds.

"By the way," said Linda, "we have a new preacher who has the Spirit within him. Don't miss the service."

Sunday is always a day when black people give themselves up entirely to their faith, but ever since this particular evangelist from Georgia had started preaching in Greenway, there had been a new outpouring of religious feeling. When Fanny entered the church where her soft voice had so often sung Baptist hymns, the benches were already filled with a grave and expectant crowd.

Then the Reverend Sandow appeared. He was a short, squat man of ordinary appearance, but his eyes burned with the flame of devotion. After reading

72

from the Scriptures, the invocation and the singing
of hymns, he rose and placed his hand on the Bible
which sat on the pulpit. Then he began to speak.
" 'Repent,' saith the Lord, 'for the kingdom of heaven
is at hand.' " This quotation stated the theme of his
sermon, though what followed seemed to have no
plan or order. Bold wit and images were followed
by praises and threats, then ludicrous clowning punc-
tuated by exaggerated gestures. He danced all along
the stage raising his arms towards heaven, pounding
the table with his fists, foaming at the mouth in a
kind of rage as the spellbound crowd responded with
"Amen!" and "Hallelujah!" The women leapt up
clapping their hands. A holy madness gripped the
congregation, transporting them to the Last Judgment
or to the mysterious shores of the Jordan. Then came
the separation of the unregenerate from the purified:
"Sinners!" he thundered, "How dare you mingle with
God's servants? Confess! Repent! Let the chaff be
separated from the grain. All those who have not let
Christ into their hearts, all those who have not received His Grace, step to the aisle on the left."
Defying shame, men and women, boys and girls,
especially those whose sins were publicly known, got
up from their seats and moved to the side of the
damned. Prayers for them arose from the rest of the
congregation, growing louder until one or another of
the sinners would cry: "I repent! I'm saved!"

For a moment Fanny thought of joining them. They
said she had failed in her duty as a wife. She wanted
to humiliate herself and beg forgiveness. But her
conscience held her back. She did not feel guilty.
She had done what she thought was right. But those
around her were looking at her almost malevolently
as though scandalized to see her among them. Her

73

visit had revived the gossip that had surrounded her departure. Martha Bledsoe had pictured her as a flighty little girl attracted by the big city, who just wanted to have a good time without worrying about her sick husband.

At the end of the service the crowd assembled on the porch in front of the church. Fanny expected to be cornered and asked all kinds of questions, but instead her old acquaintances turned away from her, as though by agreement. Of all of them, only two or three recognized her with a brusque "Hello, Fanny." Disheartened, she went back to the cabin.

She wanted to pack her bag and leave the strangers around her immediately; she wanted to go back to Boston where her friends were. But she was sure to hurt Mr. Lewis in doing so. The obedient pupil was still afraid of displeasing him.

During the next three days she felt as though she were a prisoner in a foreign land. It was understood that Linda and Mr. Lewis did not want her, though they still did not say so. They spoke neither warmly nor harshly to her, and this indifference was proof that an abyss had opened up between them for good. However, she forced herself to speak and to smile. "Don't you sing anymore?" Mr. Lewis asked her once. She sang "Grandfather's Clock" to him, but in her heart the notes were flat and without resonance.

Thursday arrived and she took her leave of Linda and Mr. Lewis, who were polite and cool to the end. "Don't worry," she told them, "we will continue to take care of you. And as the boys make more money, we will send you more."

She started back down the road to Wildwood; and though uncertainty lingered in her heart, she was relieved. As she was walking, she heard a noise. She turned to see Charlie Ross coming towards her.

"I knew from the beginning that you were here," he said, "and I know how they've treated you. But don't pay it any attention; they're all fools."

"Charlie!" Fanny said with surprise. She was happy to see him. At that moment he seemed to be her only friend.

"Yeah, it's me. I wanted to see you. Let me carry your bag. So your old husband doesn't want you anymore? You're lucky. Why did you come back to bury yourself in this awful hole?"

"I didn't come for the pleasure, Charlie; you know that."

"Yeah, yeah, I saw what you were doing." He looked at her sideways with a desirous but playful look in his eye. "One thing I can say, Fanny, you don't get any older. You look the same as you did in school when we fought under the old chestnut tree. But I bet I could throw you to the ground now with a couple of blows."

"I'd like to see you try," said Fanny, laughing. "Only, at the moment I have a lot of other things to think about."

"Yeah, you think too much, Fanny. Me, I don't think about anything — except a lot about you. Do you know how boring it is here? That old preacher has stolen all the girls."

"Well, convert. Then you would have saints for friends."

"Hm! They won't even let you smoke. Too much holiness for me. By the way," he continued, "are you ready for those two kisses?"

"Crazy man. What kisses?"

"The ones you've owed me for twenty years."

"I don't't owe you anything. A person doesn't

75

owe anything to a thief."

"That's all right; that's fine. You'll give them to me someday."

He laughed but it was evident that he meant it, and that he wanted others besides, as interest on the long-standing debt.

They walked side by side to the station. It was like a return to a long bygone day that had quickly come and gone.

"You know," he said as he was leaving, "if some-body in Boston needs a pair of strong arms, let me know."

XX

Fanny returned to her sons with a free conscience. She had offered herself in sacrifice and had been rejected. But her children's joy took away the bitterness of her unsuccessful journey. She said nothing to them of her disappoinment. She simply explained that Mr. Lewis did not want for anything and that he preferred to remain in Linda's hands. They began once more to live in the same busy, carefree manner.

Then Fanny remembered the promise that she had made to Mrs. Sidney. She owed a visit to her neighbor on the first floor, and she had offered to help her clean her apartment. One day she heard her shaking out her dust mops and moving chairs. When she arrived she found the woman in the midst of cleaning. Her large apartment took up the entire front of the building. Fanny was surprised at its opulence. In the living room there were armchairs with springs and an upholstered couch. In each of the other rooms there was a spacious bed covered with clean white sheets, a dresser with a mirror and framed pictures on the wall. She formed a high opinion of her neighbor when she saw, decorating the entrance, a beautiful hanging of pink wool embellished with metal spangles which read: "God sees all."

"I'm happy that you have come back," said Mrs. Sidney. "Without you the building seemed empty. As you see, my place is not too bad. These young girls are difficult. They have to have lavish bedrooms and a room for music. There are four staying with me at the moment and they have a lot of company. When they stay up till all hours having fun, it's a job afterwards to clean up. One of the girls who was at your party helps me with my cleaning, but she left yesterday and she'll be gone for two days. I have to wait on the others, Lord knows, but of course they pay me for it. I hope you'll meet all of them soon. They're good girls, always happy; you don't get bored here."

"Well," said Fanny, "I would be pleased to help you while the other girl is gone. I hardly have a thing to do today."

"It's not necessary to do so much," said Mrs. Sidney, "though if you would like to help me dust a little bit, why, I wouldn't refuse it. But you could do me an even bigger favor. I don't know if I can ask it of you."

"Oh, my goodness," said Fanny, "whatever you like."

"Well then: I promised someone that I would introduce him to one of the girls. He complains of being

77

lonely and he expects to see her this afternoon. But as you see they've all gone and won't be back until tonight. If he comes while you're here, would you like to welcome him and talk with him a while?"

Fanny was dumbfounded; it was a type of service that she had never encountered. She found it funny and absurd.

"But my dear," she objected, "it wouldn't be the same thing. The young man is looking for a friend. Meeting me won't bring him any nearer to having one."

"It doesn't matter. Amuse him. Help him pass the time. That's what they want, you know that. And you could do it better than anybody else."

"If it's just a question of talking, that won't be too difficult. And you have a record player; maybe he likes music. Really," she concluded, "I don't know. But if he comes, bring him in. Out of friendship for you, I'll do my best. Then your girls all have jobs?"

"Yes. Most of the time. One of them does ironing for a Chinese laundry. The others do cleaning or watch children. But they have their nights and Sundays free. Without their boyfriends, you understand, they couldn't make ends meet. Even so, they have to have more than one at a time sometimes. You have to take care of yourself the best way you can, don't you think? The one who works for me has a child — he's not legitimate, I'm afraid. If she were here, I wouldn't have to bother you. Unless, of course, you like to make friends."

"Oh, I'm quite sociable," said Fanny, naively, "but I don't have the time."

"But you never know what's going to happen. Wait, at least, and see if you like him."

78

"Hand me the duster, Mrs. Sidney. First of all, we have to give him a clean place to sit."

Despite all that had been said, Fanny, as trusting as ever, suspected nothing of the dubious character of what she was being asked to do. It was an amusing game and nothing more. But as soon as Fanny had begun to dust, Mrs. Sidney went quickly out of the back door to a nearby drugstore and made a telephone call. "John," she said in a whisper to the person at the other end, "are you free for an hour or two? There's a very charming girl with me at the moment, the one I spoke to you about. You understand? Good. Then, we'll look for you soon."

Twenty minutes later John was introduced to Fanny. She smiled at him as they shook hands.

"I'll leave you alone," said Mrs. Sidney. "I still have a lot of cleaning to do."

Fanny looked at her "guest" with interest. He was a large, well-built man in his thirties; he was nicely dressed and seemed to be polite.

"Miss," he began.

"It's 'Mrs.', sir," Fanny interrupted. "Let's get to know each other. You are no doubt married yourself," she continued.

"I . . . uh, I was . . . but, right now . . . you see . . ."

"I understand. Your wife has left you, or maybe she doesn't love you anymore, and you're lonely. Oh, how I understand that! You're looking at someone whose husband doesn't want her any longer."

"Then, maybe fate has brought us together. Mrs. Sidney said that you were nice, but I didn't think you were so young and pretty. You can't be over twenty-three."

"Add one or two more," said Fanny humorously. "You know," she went on, "that I'm just taking the

79

place of the girl Mrs. Sidney promised you.''

"What? But wasn't it you . . .''

"No, no, she's away. I'm supposed to entertain you while she's gone.''

"Are you serious? Mrs. Sidney told you that?'' asked John incredulously.

"Certainly. That's how I understand it. Is that all right?''

John was astounded at first, but when he spoke it was with an agreeable voice. "I had hoped for something else," he said, "but we can work it out. What kind of entertainment are you going to give me?''

"Let me take care of that," said Fanny. "First of all, come sit near me, and take my hand as if we were serious. Now, tell me about yourself; what worries you have, and why you and your wife couldn't get along.''

"This is some game. But, after all, why not?'' thought John.

He spoke of himself for a quarter of an hour and, surprisingly, he felt relieved. This young woman whom he hardly knew actually showed sympathy for him; her remarks were kind, and her laughter was pleasant to hear.

"In a way you are right, and in a way you are wrong," she concluded. "Your wife is not a bad person. The two of you ought to go back together. But forget all that for now. Do you like music? Do you dance?''

"A little, like everybody else," said John.

"But I bet you don't know all the dances from the South. This is one you hardly ever see here.''

She wound the phonograph and began a dance that came from the humorous and ironic soul of black people, one of those "swings" done around the cabins at night in the moonlight, full of catlike leaps, sinuous writhings and extravagant gestures. John followed her movements intently.

"But it takes two to dance to that," said Fanny. "I'll show you how."

She gave him a lesson. He caught on quickly and soon the two of them were moving around the room from corner to corner, now together, now apart, following the lively tempo of the music. Mrs. Sidney could feel the force of their steps through her kitchen floor.

Out of breath, John gasped: "Well, Miss or Mrs., you certainly can move!"

"I can do a lot better than that," said Fanny. "A somersault used to be nothing for me. Do you know how to do a real somersault?"

"That I can do, yes," said John, straightening. "There's nobody better than me on the athletic field."

"Then try one. I'll watch."

Alarmed, John said: "But, you don't really mean . . ."

"Why, of course. Aren't we having fun?

John looked at her uncertainly, piqued by her challenge. Then, suddenly, he leaped into the air and executed a perfect somersault. Mrs. Sidney was somewhat startled when he landed.

"Not too bad," said Fanny. "Gracious, I wish I were dressed for it." Tempted, she looked at her dress and then took hold of its sides, ready to leap. Finally, though, she restrained herself.

"You're lucky that I'm in no position to do one. You would have seen how we jump where I come from," she said. "I can run, too, believe me, and climb trees." They both laughed.

"Good Lord. You're not twenty-five," said John,

"you're closer to sixteen or seventeen."

"I've been seventeen all my life," Fanny conceded. "Anyhow, we could be a pair of acrobats." Caught up in her own game, Fanny was enjoying herself immensely. She began to hum a popular love song. "Singing, that's another thing I like to do," she said. So they sang "Old Black Joe" together, and "Oh, Suzanna," and some songs that were then popular in Boston.

John was delighted with his companion, it was as though a whirlwind had seized him. He had even forgotten why he had come.

"Now," said Fanny, "you're probably ready for some orangeade and cookies. After that, I'll have to go." Before he could reply, she had left the kitchen.

"Heavens above!" Mrs. Sidney exclaimed, looking at her slyly, "what have you been up to in there for the past two hours?"

"I've been entertaining him," Fanny replied. She returned with a tray and glasses; she was as polite and pleasing as a young girl at her first dance.

"A person certainly doesn't get bored with you around," John said with conviction. Then, recovering a little, he said: "I hope there will be another time."

"Next time you'll be with your friend," Fanny said. "Good evening, and good luck. It would surprise you to learn that I have three grown children." She left him stunned and went to see Mrs. Sidney with a smile upon her face. "Ask him if I haven't kept him busy," she said.

When she had left, John, now returned to normal, went to Mrs. Sidney and said, "She's a real demon, that girl! She wraps you around her little finger like a thread. Sure, she showed me a good time, but how do you figure, that in the end, I didn't even think of asking

82

her for a kiss!"

Fanny reflected, also, on her experience. "What sort of way is that," she asked herself, "to entertain people? It must be the style here in Boston." Then she continued to clean and peel her vegetables, and thought no more about it.

XXI

"After that," continued Maude Olliver, "they put me to work in a cotton mill. Then I went to work for a woman who was half-crippled, and since I lived with her, I was kind of free. My husband was trying to see me again, as you would imagine. We would meet each other, and I even went to where he lived. No one knew of it. But the poor boy got sick and had to leave New Bedford. I have since learned that he died a year later. I was tormented because I was afraid of 'you-know-what.' But I found a woman doctor who took care of me for twenty-five dollars.

"I went to work then on a line of ships that sailed along the coast between New York and Miami. I cleaned cabins and waited on tables. The tips were good. The supervisor was drunk from morning to night and let us do what we wanted.

"During a stopover, the coal barge which refueled us was docked alongside, and a fellow on the bridge called out to me:

'Hello there,' he said, 'aren't you Maude Olliver?'

'That's me. How do you know?' I asked.

'Don't you remember dancing with me at the sailor's ball in Norfolk?' I didn't really remember, but it was possible. 'Come on over and talk a while,' he said.

"I didn't have anything to do so I went up the gangplank and we stood with our elbows on the rail talking like two old friends. He was the barge's captain. He traveled from Maine to Florida loading and unloading coal for companies.

'Where are you from?' I asked him.

'The same place as you,' he said. 'I come from New Bedford. But I left three years ago. Maybe you know my cousin Fernandez?' I knew him. He was a West Indian who ran a grocery store.

'Listen,' he said, 'you made such an impression on me at that dance that I asked about you later. We'll have to meet again. We go our own ways tomorrow and we'll be traveling quite a bit. But on the twenty-second of September, our ships will both be in New York. When you come ashore I'll be waiting for you.'

'Yes, we'll see each other again,' I said, 'if you're there.' I didn't really expect him to be.

"But he was there, just as he said. He took me to his sister's. There was a brother living with them as well. They gave me a cordial welcome, and when, a week later, he asked me to marry him, they had no objections. I couldn't believe it. He was big and good-looking, he made a lot of money, and he was respected by everyone. He was very obliging towards me; he was kind, he was all you could wish. 'Take one last trip,' he said, 'and when you come back everything will be ready.' And he gave me a diamond ring that cost a hundred dollars.

"Fifteen days later, when I returned, I found more

than I had hoped for. He had rented a beautiful apartment. There was furniture of all kinds, even an inlaid tea-tray with wheels and a buffet covered with silver and dishes. I believe that every West Indian in New York was at our wedding, not counting a lot of friends from New Bedford. The house was full of company for eight days, and there was enough whiskey for an army.

"Afterwards, he had to go back to his ship. I would have gone back to work, too, but he wouldn't hear of it. I saw him once or twice a month when he came into New York; sometimes, they would put in for two or three days. Mrs. Lewis, I loved that man, and he deserved it. His sister would visit me, but, still, I was so bored while he was gone that I finally told him, 'Listen, Dessie, I want to be with you. Take me with you and I'll help you. You can let one of your two seamen go, if you want; I know the sea as well as they do.' He was as pleased to have me as I was to be with him, so we left together. I've never been as happy as I was then on board that barge. It was our kingdom. We had fresh air to breathe, beautiful scenery to look at along the coast, and the sea was always changing; it would rise up in swells to shake us and force us to keep our eyes open. There were some pretty big storms, too. I would be on the bridge with the others helping to lower the anchor and taking the wheel. Back in our cabin at night, following behind a tugboat, we felt as though we owned the world and were the only people in it. Twice we delivered coal as far as Bermuda. He had been born farther south in the Grenadines on the little island of Bequia, and he spoke to me of his mother who was still living there. 'We'll go to see her one of these days,' he said.

"I led that life for three years and four months, and I would like to be leading it still. We were close to each other all the time, as much as in the early days."

Maude, unconsciously, reached for her handkerchief as if to wipe a tear which was not going to flow, but which burned inside her all the same.

XXII

The New African Review lasted only three months. From the first it was meant to be the equal of the large American magazines. It was carefully and elaborately designed and offered intelligent, well-written articles. Edward had assembled a group of writers which would have honored any academy. But the question of money spoiled everything. The rare subscriptions were not sufficient to pay expenses and the printer refused to carry the magazine any longer. Not only was his dream destroyed, but he had assumed obligations that he was unable to meet. Foolishly optimistic, he had accepted payment for one- and two-year and even lifetime subscriptions. In demanding what was owed them, Edward was aware, the subscribers could cause him a lot of trouble. Disappointed but calm, he said to Fanny. "I see now what we should have done. We should have gotten ourselves a press and done our own work without depending on anybody else. That's what I aim to do. The magazine will exist again before long, and we'll be able to satisfy everybody, even if we're a little late. I'll send a letter telling them of the plan. If some refuse, then I'll pay them out of my own pocket.''

Few of them took the trouble to refuse, but five or six complained to the postal authorities that they suspected a swindle. Edward had to furnish his employers with embarrassing explanations, and was severely reprimanded. They had strict rules where the behavior of their employees was concerned, and the incident was recorded as a mark against him.

At the end of a month, using all his wages and some money that he had borrowed, Edward bought some type and set up an old press in an abandoned basement. He obtained it with a small deposit and a promise of monthly payments. He was unable to help the family financially now. ''Do your best,'' Fanny told him, ''and get back on your feet. We'll do what we can in the meantime.'' He spent his evenings learning his new trade. Composing stick in hand, he worked laboriously assembling the lines of his opening article. He worked passionately, believing that when he had mastered the techniques, he would have more than one way to make money. ''Think of the millions of letter-heads, programs, cards and announcements that are printed every day. A small part of that would be enough to keep me afloat; the magazine will sail under its own steam.''

His collaborators however, felt let down and turned their backs on him. He no longer got money for ink and paper, the rent for the basement or for the salary of the helper whom he had been forced to hire. Despite all these difficulties, he succeeded in printing a sixteen-page magazine, in which he wrote, ''Let our friends have patience. The *Review* will live. We will fulfill our promises.'' But the magazine died.

There was now the problem of finding a use for the press. "Obviously," Edward said, "our people are not yet concerned about serious art. We'll have to give them what they want." Slowly a plan took shape in his mind which he thought to be foolproof. He would create a purely practical magazine which would open the doors of success to people by offering them simple ways to make money: businesses that needed no capital, little known methods of manufacture, small jobs that could be done at home, opportunities to sell new inventions or books in private editions, and hundreds of other sure secrets for making a fortune quickly. He thought, also, of the number of people, young and old, who spent their lives in search of companionship. He would be providing a public service in putting them in touch with each other across great distances. But the real novelty of the enterprise was that he himself ran no risk, for sales and advertisements alone would support the magazine. All those looking for friends and fortunes would have to pay twenty-five cents to have their requests or projects printed. No number of the magazine would appear until enough money was available to pay for it. Women, however, would not be asked to pay their calls for companions would be a major attraction to males. Furthermore, this time he would not appeal to black people only, but to all races in all countries. He would call the magazine *The Universal Exchange*.

"But who is going to read it?" Fanny objected.

"It's simple. All exchangers will be given a copy each and the rest will go to newsstands in all the big cities."

"How are you going to find so many lonely people?"

"Again, it's simple. To start with I'll go to the telephone book and take down a hundred or so names of women who live alone. I'll get others from return addresses on envelopes where I'm working. Then I'll send a circular out to all of them offering my services free of charge. Think of the number of people who will take me up on it."

"Hm! And what takers! But, these 'free services...'"

"I know, I know, I don't get anything out of it. It means that the first month I won't have anything to depend on except the advertisements. But, once I get it going..."

"You're full of ideas, son," said Fanny, caressing his shoulder. "If you keep trying, you're bound to find one that will work." But, sadly, she doubted it.

XXIII

A short time later, Mr. Lewis died. Linda found him one morning, cold and already rigid on the floor near his bed. The paralysis in his limbs had reached his heart. The family was shocked and saddened. His sons had always admired their father's learning and calm wisdom, and were still attached to him. Fanny lost the god and teacher of her childhood to whom she had remained faithful. She cried bitterly in spite of the painful memories which he had left her. But she was afraid to confront the hostile people who would gather at his coffin, so Frank went to Greenway to pay their final respects. By chance he encountered his brother Robert, whose travels were bringing him through the village. He was taller and stronger and had no complaints either about the world or his fellow man. Homeless, without worries, he went wherever fate led him. Nothing could convince him to live with his brothers, but he asked Frank to take back to his mother a rare shell and some gold nuggets which he had found in a river in Idaho.

XXIV

George was the only one of the three brothers who was reserved with his mother. The others hid nothing from Fanny, but George, despite his affection for her, lived his life in secret. He did not tell her when he changed jobs, but she knew that he had joined a jazz band. He no longer turned over his entire salary to her, and he came home late at night with only vague excuses as to where he had been. When Fanny asked him gently if he had a girl friend, he replied, "Don't ask so many questions, mama. I'm not a child any more. I do like everybody else."

One night about nine o'clock, Fanny was working alone in the kitchen when from the street she heard an unusual racket as of a large automobile stopping, and then a confusion of shouts. Believing it to be a traffic jam, she paid no further attention. Just then Mrs. Rollins ran downstairs and knocked several times at Fanny's door.

"Do you know what's happening, Mrs. Lewis?" she cried excitedly.

"My goodness, no," said Fanny. "What's happening?"

"The police are raiding Mrs. Sidney's!"

They hurried to a window from which they could see everything. The patrol wagon was parked in front of the building and was blocking the street, and there was already a large, barely manageable crowd standing around it. There were five policemen, each grappling with a hysterical young woman who tried obstinately to drive her pointed heels into his shins. One by one they were placed in the wagon. Then the policemen reentered the building and emerged escorting three men who, aside from cursing vigorously, offered no resistance. They, too, were locked inside the narrow van and then all were hurriedly driven away from the tense and shouting crowd.

"It had to happen," said Mrs. Rollins. "Sidney's been running that business for too long a time."

"I didn't suspect it until eight days ago," Fanny said. "All the same, the poor girls — it's tough for them."

"They have jobs, too; and one of them had a baby in her arms."

"What will they do to them?" Fanny asked.

"Oh, they'll get off with a fine. But the madam will get six months, maybe; and the house will be closed. By the way, did you recognize any of the men?"

"No, their backs were turned. But one of them looked very young."

"I'm leaving now," said Mrs. Rollins. "I'm going to tell Irene. She didn't hear a thing, I'm sure."

Alone, Fanny's thoughts returned to her recent introduction to the strange world below her. So it was one of those "houses" of which people spoke so much. And the same John whom she had "entertained," he was certainly one of the three to be put in the wagon. She shuddered to think that the other day she could have been carried away with him and locked in a cage. "But, if he never did more than he did with me . . ." she reflected.

She sat down and began to sew while she waited for her sons to return. Edward, and then Frank, came home; both were surprised when they heard the news. Time passed. "George is very late," Fanny remarked. "You know how he is," Edward said. "It's pointless to wait up for him. He'll find his way back to the nest." Still, Fanny wanted to wait for him, but her sons made her go to bed. She slept fitfully, unable to rid her mind of what she had seen in the street.

The next morning, she went directly to George's door and knocked. After a moment she uttered a short cry — her son had not come home at all. She rushed to wake Frank and Edward. "My God," she moaned. "What could have happened to him?" The two boys looked at each other uncomfortably, afraid that they knew what had happened.

"Mama," said Frank, "it could be that he worked all night. I'll go to find out. Don't fret."

But Fanny was grief-stricken. She imagined the worst, and her worry increased with each passing minute. Finally, around eleven o'clock, from her spot at the window where she was keeping anxious watch she saw her son turn the corner onto the street. He looked safe and sound. But he was not alone. At his side walked a woman with a baby in her arms.

Fanny was puzzled and surprised, but, most of all, she was happy. She went to the door and stood ready to open it. A few moments later George appeared with one of the girls whom the police had dragged out of Mrs. Sidney's; she had been at the party, also. Her name was Celia.

George looked morose and embarrassed, but the young girl seemed at ease. Her round, comely face, framed by hair still disheveled from the previous night, looked stubborn and defiant as she stood erect but casual, holding her baby in one arm like an ordinary package, and surveyed the room.

"Mama," said George, "you know what happened to me. I was at court and had to pay a fine. I know it's not very nice, but what's done is done. This is Celia. She doesn't know a soul, and she's got no place to go. I'd like you to let her stay here a while. She's a friend of mine."

This revelation and this request were crushing blows. She saw clearly the steps which had led her son to this impasse. She now had a difficult and dangerous decision to make.

"Those damn' cops," said Celia. "They can't leave you alone. As though a girl didn't have enough trouble making a living!"

Fanny looked at both of them. Young, blind, rejected and with no place to go, despite their brave front, they needed help and were asking her for it. She pitied her son, and because of him, she felt sympathy for his friend, though she was frightened by her at the same time.

"Come in, then," she said. Not daring to think of what her decision might lead to, she was following her heart as she had always done. "We have a vacant room, Celia," she continued. "This is it. Make

93

yourself at home."

"Gosh, it's swell of you to do this," said Celia. "George had told me... Honey, do you want to help me get settled?"

"Thank you, mama," said George, embracing his mother. Then he followed Celia into the room. For a short time Fanny could hear the baby whining, then he grew calm.

XXV

The family's serene and intimate life, which had revolved heretofore around Fanny, was seriously disturbed by the young woman's arrival. From the first she acted as if the apartment were her own, talking incessantly and in a loud voice, and taking over the kitchen to cook and wash for her child. Her rude clamor rang in every room. Further, she seemed to have unlimited power over George. His brothers were apprehensive lest he should be seriously in love with her. Soon, however, they themselves were attracted by her, charmed by her smiles and amorous glances.

But Fanny could not rest easy in such an equivocal situation. For her son's sake, she would have consented to step aside, just as she had done for Martha Bledsoe, but she was afraid that it might lead to his ruin.

"George," she said, "tell me, seriously. Is this child yours?"

"To tell you the truth, mama, I don't know for sure," he replied. "But I don't think so. Even Celia doesn't know."

"Then you're not obliged to take care of her? You could get rid of her and go back to the life you had before you met her?"

"I could, mama, but I like her too much to turn her out like that. When she has somewhere else to go . . ."

"Then help her to find a place. You know that, personally, I have nothing against her, but I'm worried about your future."

Some days later, and undoubtedly at George's suggestion, Celia made a proposal to Fanny. "Don't think," she said, "that it suits me to sit around and do nothing, Mrs. Lewis. I'd like to be able to work and scrape together a little money. But how can I with the child? Do you see any way for me to be free? Unless you would keep him for me, but I don't know if you would find that possible. Naturally, I'd pay you whatever was necessary. I'd pay you rent then, too."

Fanny felt a shiver of disgust. After so many years, how could she again agree to spend her days taking care of a child? How could she accept this new slavery? But how else could she free Celia — and, thus, George?

"It wouldn't be for long, would it?" she asked.

"I sure hope not," said Celia. "But, anyway, I'll be paying you rent."

"Frankly, we're not that interested in having boarders," Fanny replied. "But you deserve a helping hand until you can be independent. Find a job. I'll take care of your child. And don't worry about the money. We'll make an arrangement."

Celia soon found a job. She said that she was

working in a restaurant. What was certain was that she left the apartment each morning and did not return till evening. Also, she seemed to want for nothing. Fanny was surprised by the kinds of clothes that she wore to work, and by her new dresses. Soon she was acting even more freely with the boys. She asked them to play cards with her. They would smoke cigarettes and joke with each other, occasionally breaking into laughter over some word spoken in a low voice.

During the day when she was alone with the child, Fanny thought sadly of her new role. Inwardly she was jealous of her sons and of Celia. They were free, as she was not, to seek pleasure; yet, she was as full of life as they were, she knew better than they did the meaning of real joy. But she was rocking another woman's child, and singing him the song that she had sung to her own sons:

In watching its pendulum swing to and fro,
Many hours had he spent while a boy;
And in childhood and manhood the clock seemed to
know
And to share both his grief and his joy.
For it struck twenty-four when he entered at the door,
With a booming and beautiful pride;
But it stopped short — never to go again—
When the old man died.

Ninety years without slumbering (tick-tock, tick-
tock),
His life seconds numbering (tick-tock, tick-tock).

At those times memories of Mr. Lewis and Linda, Greenway, her lost childhood, and her stifled youth would come back to her.

One day, Frank pulled her aside and said: "Mama, I don't want to gossip, but this Celia is really something. She doesn't care about anyone. George doesn't know the kind of work she's doing, but I found out. She's a dancer at the 'Merry Africa' nightclub. You know, it has a bad reputation. I don't care myself; it's for George. And listen to this. She's trying to seduce both me and Edward. Wouldn't it be fine if she turned us against each other! For me, there's no danger, but I'm worried about Edward. I wish she would leave us alone."

"I wish so, too, Frank, more than you," said Fanny with a sigh. "But I don't dare... Let's have a little more patience."

Two months passed without trouble. Then, one morning when she had risen early, Fanny spied Edward coming quietly out of Celia's room. At first she was too shocked to speak or even to move, but, recovering before he noticed her, she stepped quickly into a corner of the room where she could not be seen. Later, she served breakfast to her sons as usual, and they left for work unaware that anything was wrong. But when the girl appeared, she said bluntly: "Celia, I'm sorry, but you can't stay here any longer. You'll have to go."

"What? What's the problem? Cops after me again?"

"No, but the 'cops' didn't teach you anything. You don't know how to act with people who want to help you."

"What have I done wrong?" she asked. Then she realized why Fanny was angry. "Well, listen, it's not my fault if your boys fall for me and run after me all the time."

"The way you act with them — and with a lot of others, too — is very wrong."

"Oh, is that so? The way I act with them. I act the same way you acted with John. Remember? You think I don't know your little secret? Mrs. Sidney told me all about it. And, by God, I'll tell George, I'll tell anybody who'll listen. You're no better than anyone else! Yes, I'm going — and right now!"

She went into her room, slamming the door behind her, leaving Fanny angry and despondent. Fifteen minutes later the girl departed without a word, her child in one arm and a package containing her clothes in the other.

That night Fanny waited for George in vain. After leaving, Celia had gone to him and he stayed with her in an apartment which she had rented. The next day a note came, telling Fanny of his decision. She sensed from his tone that he believed what the girl had told him. He ended by saying that he would always be close to her, but that he was determined to lead his own life and to share it with the one he loved.

First Edward, and then Frank went to him and asked him to come home. But it was no use. Finally, Fanny herself went to see him, ready to fight, ready to beg, but Celia, who was alone at the time, saw her coming and refused to answer the door.

XXVI

This loss of a second son was very hard on Fanny.
She cried whenever she was alone; her heart was
heavy. Edward knew nothing of the part he had played in the catastrophe. She kept it from him for fear
of distressing him, and treated him with increased
tenderness. She worked steadily to help him with his
new undertaking, aware of the consequences of
George's defection. For the moment Frank was the
family's sole support. Eager for Edward to join him,
she labored, classifying advertisements full of promises and calls for affection which were mostly from
women. His mail was abundant, and came from as
far away as Austria and Australia. Once again she
allowed herself to hope that this idea would succeed.
But still her sadness did not go away. Her neighbors
saw it, and understood.

"Poor soul, you're not the same person," Mrs.
Rollins said. "You should try to throw it off. I know
what I would do in your place."

"Tell me quick, I beg you. You don't think I'm
this way because I want to be, do you?"

"Religion, Mrs. Lewis; that's the answer for all
of us. Get religion, you'll see what it will do for
you."

"But I pray to God every day," said Fanny.

"I don't doubt that, but you're too far away from
Him when you pray. You should stand in His presence and speak to Him just as I'm speaking to you.

Recently, you know, a wondrous thing took place, Father Divine himself descended among us.''

''Father Divine? Oh, yes, someone told me about him. But I don't know much about him. I thought he was in New York.''

''He's in Boston, now,'' said Mrs. Rollins. ''I was present at the opening of Heaven and received Father's blessing.''

''The opening of...? That sounds like something. But please tell me what a heaven is.''

''A heaven, well, it's the Lord surrounded by angels who are ready to do his bidding, and all the saints at the large table that he has laid out for them and singing hymns in joy and plenty.''

''That's all well and good,'' said Fanny, ''but can you find it this side of heaven?''

''It's right at your door, no farther away than Columbus Avenue. It's wonderful, my dear, simply wonderful. Already there are one hundred and thirty eight angels. And if you could see the meals that are served in that house! It's open to anyone, and it doesn't cost a cent. And when Father Divine appear to bless the meal — oh, the hallelujahs he receives the words of gratitude! And Father speaks with the brothers and sisters just like any other man would.''

Someone who did not know Mrs. Rollins better might have thought her a deluded woman who had invented a fantastic story. But she was merely describing what she had seen and what was well known. A superhuman being whose origins no one could trace, had appeared among them. He was the bearer of a new revelation, the incarnation of the heavenly Father, who brought with him peace and salvation he was visible Providence attending to the needs of soul and body — none of his children would die

100

His cult had expanded rapidly from its obscure beginnings, and among his followers were persons of all colors.

George Baker had possibly been a gardener and common laborer. Where he was born no one knew, but at twenty-five he was teaching Sunday school in Philadelphia. Leaving there, he traveled widely, causing astonishment wherever he went with his outrageous doctrines until, finally, he was declared a "lunatic" by a court in Georgia. But that was only a sign of the greatness of his mission. Jesus, also, had been a laborer; he, too, had preached along the roads and suffered persecution at the hands of men. Then the "Heavenly-Sent" knew triumph; his preaching began to attract big crowds. At Sayville, first, on Long Island, then in Harlem, he established several branches of his "kingdom." In each branch lived his "angels," holy women whom he himself had chosen. They gave him all their worldly goods and he supported them in return. All changed their names, each to be known thenceforth by a mystical title such as "Faith," "Sweetness," "Archangel," "Incense," "Hosanna," "Pure Love." They helped the Supreme Master find work for masses of unemployed people; they helped find shelter for those who had none; they fed the indigent who crowded into their dining halls. There was a single, prescribed greeting to be used everytime they met: "Peace — it's wonderful!"

Father Divine went from on Heaven to another spreading the gospel. He blessed meals and guests, and everywhere he was received with delirious welcome. At times, processions would escort him through the streets, reenacting Christ's triumphs; the avenues would resound with shouts and songs. Alarmed, the

101

authorities tried to put a stop to these processions. A judge fined the Father five hundred dollars. Four days later the judge was struck down by an aneurysm: punishment, undeniably, for his ungodly action. The all-powerful prophet was even more respected from then on. Even scoffers had to admit his good works. During an election campaign, the mayor of New York eulogized him publicly. A thousand acres of land came into the cult's possession, and dress-making shops, hairdressers' shops, all kinds of stores, farms, and two newspapers contributed to his income. None of which, moreover, was in the Father's name. His reign was not of this world. Deeds were in the names of the angels. (One of whom, alas, betrayed him, departing with her property and proclaiming that he was nothing but a "damn ordinary man.") A hundred Paradises existed now in several states, in England, Switzerland and as far as Australia. The latest, in Boston, was a huge success.

"If you want," said Mrs. Rollins, "I'll take you to a meeting. Father is supposed to come in a couple of weeks. Have faith, he will wash away your troubles as though they were dust."

"I hope so," said Fanny. "Thank you for being so kind."

She was not so sure of a happy ending. Yet, once she and her neighbor were on the road to "Heaven" her heart was seized by expectation. She would give a great deal to see the fog that enclosed her melt, and its causes vanish with it.

The meetings were held in a large hall which had once served as a haberdasher's warehouse. A raised platform dominated the back of the room. Its center was filled with long rows of painted boards supported by sawhorses. On both sides the narrow aisles were furnished with chairs. Extended along the walls were two large inscriptions which read, "Thou preparest a table before me in the presence of mine enemies," and "Praised be the Lord from whom all blessings flow." Banners and emblems decorated the walls in various places.

When the two visitors entered there were already three hundred persons seated on the benches which ran the length of the tables. The angels were moving from one table to the next, placing bowls full of hot, steaming soup at equal intervals among the bright, homely settings. Conversation was happy and animated and, frequently, eagerly expectant eyes turned towards a draped door. Fanny and Mrs. Rollins found places apart from the others and had begun to observe the scene, when suddenly the door opened and Father Divine stepped through it. Talk ended and the crowd stood up.

"Peace — it's wonderful!" The cry erupted from every bench, joined to a swell of applause. Shouts of welcome, and loving and exalted praises followed: "Glory to the Beloved Father!" "Hail the Lord, the King!" "He's beautiful! He's magnificent!" Everywhere hands were outstretched in attitudes of prayer.

The Father mounted the stage and allowed the ovation to continue for a full minute. Then, at his signal the hall fell silent. Fanny could see him clearly as he stood motionless with the light full upon him. He was short and solidly built. He carried his fifty-odd years with ease. Nothing in look or manner suggested the superhuman. If that was divinity, then one could, perhaps, sympathize with the renegade angel. But, no doubt, the man's very ordinariness was one of the things that attracted such numbers to him. His bald head and artless smile gave him the appearance of a simple guest at a family reunion. Discernible in his soft, clear brown eyes was the glint of a distant vision, but they were neither domineering nor hypnotic; like his unmannered stride, they belonged to a naive and neighborly god who had taken the image of his creatures to move among them, dispensing his gifts in just exchange for their veneration, satisfied with himself and with his universe.

He spoke with calm authority in phrases which seemed, at first, to make no sense. Filled with words that knew no dictionary, they seemed aimed beyond the understanding, at the unconscious.

"Angels and children," he began, "you have proclaimed my word. Say it again. "Peace!" "Peace — it's wonderful!" the crowd chanted. "Now, listen to what I say. My mission is of the Spirit. The Celestial Spirit is among you. It is not only materializable and visualizable, it is materialized and visualized. And I say further that it is externalified and extemporafied. Believe in it! It is come to bring you the supermental peace and relaxation of God's children, to aid you grandiosely in your need. Angels, have you prepared a table for those who serve me?" "Yes, our Father," they replied. "Amen!" the crowd sang, "Hallelujah!" "Let all eat and bless my name. Sing, rejoice, be happy in the Lord."

With loud chatter and laughter the guests sat down to eat their soup. When they had finished, the angels brought large pots full of chicken and potatoes. "Hosanna!" shouted the recipients; "Thank you, Father!" Seated at the end of one of the tables, the beneficent god presided graciously, eating the same food as they and pouring coffee for them when their cups were empty.

Fanny and her friend had come with the intention

of being merely spectators, but an angel noticed them and insisted amiably that they join the others. Responding wholeheartedly to the worshippers' enthusiasm, Fanny was soon shouting with them, "Peace — it's wonderful!" her problems, for the moment, forgotten.

When the meal was over and forks and knives and tongues were silent, Father Divine again addressed the faithful.

"Give thanks, now, to the Bestower of all gifts."

"Oh, thank you our Father! Hallelujah!" they responded.

"You see now how I provide for my own. How many are there here?"

"Three hundred!"

"Did you have enough chicken?"

"Yes, yes!"

"Did you have enough potatoes?"

"Yes, yes!"

"What did you pay for it?"

"Nothing! Amen! Hosanna!"

"It is by the divinification of supremely sanctified humanity that I provide for you."

"That's the truth! Amen!"

"Remember that peace is sweet."

"Peace is sweet!"

"Peace is praiseworthy and a hundred times praiseworthy!"

"A hundred times — A thousand times — Ten thousand times praiseworthy!"

"I will return soon. Do not forget it."

"Peace! Oh, thank you! Glory be to the beloved Father! He is beautiful! He is grand! He is magnificent!" The shouts came from all sides. Then as arms waved frantically and couples formed at random and danced hysterically, the Father, with a wave of the hand, walked out of sight, and the door was shut behind him.

Fanny was silent. What she had seen had shocked her, and her ears still rang with its echo. She had been less impressed with the miracle worker himself than with the secure, triumphant faith of his believers, their exultant and contagious joy, the peace which they proclaimed and which shone on their faces.

When they reached the street, Mrs. Rollins asked Fanny, "What did you think of it?"

"I think that it does a person good to see it, and whatever does a person good must come from on high."

"But, you don't believe that you have seen God himself?"

She would have answered, "Yes, perhaps", but the shadow of Mr. Lewis and his teaching kept her from it.

"I'm not ready," she said, "to worship Father Divine, but I thank him for having comforted me. Thank you, too, Mrs. Rollins. Come tell me often that 'Peace — it's wonderful!' "

XXVII

Edward's new enterprise had grown rapidly at first.
He had correctly judged the attraction offered by the
combination of emotion and commerce. Advertisements and appeals for correspondence sat next to each
other on the pages of his magazine: "Iowa inventor
has ingenious can opener for sale;" "A young girl
in Basses-Pyrénées, educated, affectionate, wishes to
correspond with distinguished young American who
has knowledge of French;" "We are looking for
agents to sell a sock-darning device;" "Russian noble-
man speaking seven languages, ruined by revolution,
would like to make acquaintance of a lady of means;"
Stamp collectors will profit from writing to the under-
signed;" "Teacher in Berlin wishes to improve
her English through an exchange of letters;" "Do you
want to get rich? Distribute my cure for chicken
cholera;" "Young ladies! Write to me! I am a sober,
honest, industrious farmer with six hundred dollars
in the bank;" "Unemployed painter desires work
restoring faded signs;" "Belgian actress, blonde,
invites young man between sixteen and thirty-five,
with a loving nature to write her, expressing himself familiarly and with an open heart;" "Burial-
Provision Society offers its clients decent funerals at
lowest possible rates;" and so forth.

Edward and Fanny were hopeful. But one evening
a letter came, which read: "Edward Lewis, Sorter,
employee number 504, is asked to present himself

tomorrow morning, Thursday, at the director's office, for a matter which concerns him. Stanwick.''

''What can they want with you?'' asked Fanny.

''No doubt, something to do with the job.''

But she said to herself that it was the first time such a thing had happened. She remained worried until Edward returned home the next day. The serene look on his face reassured her.

''What was it?'' she asked.

''Nothing at all, really. You'll never believe it, but they object to my magazine. According to the director, he has been flooded with complaints. A sixty-year old widow was shocked when she received one of our circulars. 'Just where did they get my name?' she wanted to know. Somebody else, on the strength of one of our advertisements, sent a dollar for ten yards of silk and claims she got embroidery thread instead. Then the director was suspicious of the advertisements offering books 'forbidden to the public,' and of another from a photographer who wanted 'broad-minded, well-shaped models.' 'A minister brought that one to show me,' he said. 'But, sir,' I said, 'I'm not responsible for every one of my advertisers. If they break the law, let them be arrested.' 'But you are responsible for the good name of our employees,' he said. 'I've already warned you to stop this silly business. Either you smarten up or you're fired.' Isn't that high-handed? So, you see — I'm free.''

''No, I don't see,'' said Fanny weakly.

''Think about it. You don't imagine that I hesitated a second in choosing between a growing business and some sorry little job!''

Fanny was appalled to hear that her son would give up a secure career for the uncertainty of his magazine. ''Shouldn't you have thought about it?'' she asked.

"But mama," Edward said, "I had thought about it. For some time already I've felt overworked and have thought of devoting myself strictly to the *Exchange*."

To talk about it was useless, Fanny knew. The damage was irreparable. She retired quickly to her room and, no longer able to restrain herself, she covered the sounds of her disappointment with her pillow.

XXVIII

When she got up from the bed, she knew that there was but one way out for them, and she was resolved to take it. Obviously she could never again count on Edward. The *Exchange*, despite its apparent success, was barely paying for itself and could fail any day. It was left to Frank to provide for them all, which she did not want. She herself would work anywhere, at anything, to help him.

She was still classifying the *Exchange*'s advertisements, and did it so well that Edward printed them without rereading them. The next day she inserted into the copy a paragraph of her own which read: "Middle-aged colored woman, hard worker, accommodating, expert housekeeper, seeking work for a few hours a day. Terms to be discussed. Contact F.L., c/o *Exchange*." Then, a few days later, she could hear the beating of her heart as she opened the magazine and found her notice. Her sons had not seen it.

A week went by bringing no response. She had

begun to lose hope when, one day, among a pile of letters she saw one addressed to "F.L." Feverishly, almost dropping it, she opened the letter to read: "Madam, I could provide employment for the person you describe. I am a man living alone. I work in an office and have need of a housekeeper. If you will please inform me of your address, as well as with the day and hour at which I could meet you, I will come in the hope of reaching an agreement. Donat Sylvain, 50 Commonwealth Avenue."

Then Fanny read the letter again, overjoyed and intrigued. Unable to keep her pleasure to herself, she went upstairs to the third floor to see Irene. Her neighbor was busy combing her hair.

"Read this," Fanny said. "What do you make of it? Do you think there's a chance that this man will hire me?"

Irene ran her lone eye over the page. "Of course there's a chance," she said. "Why would he have written? And there's no one more capable than you."

"But I hadn't considered working for a single man," said Fanny.

"They're the ones who need housekeepers, aren't they? This isn't any ordinary man, either, believe you me."

"What? How do you know?"

"I see everything right here in this paper. First of all, he's white; that's obvious. You don't think black people live on Commonwealth Avenue, do you? And he's a gentleman. Listen, 'If you will please inform me . . .', ' . . . in the hope of reaching an agreement . . .' Damn! What politeness. Most other people would have written, 'Concerning your advertisement, I'll expect you with your brushes.' He's well off, at the least. You don't live in that corner of town on

110

peanuts. He's educated, no question of that. Look at his nice handwriting. And he tells you that he works in an office.''

"Is that all," said Fanny, laughing.

"No. What's more, he's a Frenchman."

"French!" Fanny exclaimed. The fact made her employer more distant than ever.

"Sure. 'Sylvain' is a French name. In a hotel in Cleveland where I worked as a maid, there was a man staying there who was called that. But, don't let it bother you. French people are no worse than anybody else, all things considered."

"I don't care, really," said Fanny. "Working for this one or that one is all the same to me."

XXIX

As Irene had guessed, and for reasons which she could not know, Donat Sylvain was not at all "any ordinary man."

Outwardly, his life seemed normal. He illustrated books for a publishing house, and in his spare time drew portraits for a small number of clients. But anyone knowing his past would have seen there the traces of an unusual personality, and of destiny's caprice.

He was a man of contrasts. At once naturally taciturn and retiring, open and sympathetic, his timid coolness hid a passionate heart. Frank and honest when dealing with the world, he was surprised not to be able

111

to follow conventional paths and to end up always isolated from others. Quick to give himself, his heart was both weak and constant; he was easily made a prisoner of impulsive love and imprudent pity. Sensitive to the slightest injury, he was incapable of rancor or vengeance. In sum, he was a man poorly adapted to life's struggles, a person too soft for the violence life demands; he was by nature one made to suffer all the shocks of a world where the hard and aggressive alone go unscathed.

After a cloistered and protected childhood, after an ascetic youth spent immured behind school walls, he made yet another prison for himself. Following his inclinations, he fled society and engrossed himself in studies which led to no practical end. He tried several different occupations and was discouraged and disgusted by them all. But with his sojourn in America, he seemed to have reached a definite stage in his life. At thirty-seven, he was an artist infatuated with beauty, a thinker without illusions, a tranquil skeptic, a man weary from so many lives already lived.

In recent days he had lived more than ever alone nursing the wound inflicted upon him by a companion of three years whom he had trusted with childlike faith. Showing no emotion or any visible regret, she had left one morning without explanation. But he knew why she had left. She begrudged him his meditative instincts, his hermit's ways, the hours spent drawing or writing poetry, his ignorance or contempt for convention. If she had loved him, what would these things have mattered? But she hankered after pleasure and excitement. She was like a transparent bubble that needed to soar, to mirror the sun. She, as he, had to follow her nature. He understood and forgave her, and that made her repudiation of him even more

112

difficult to bear.

Since, he had lived in complete solitude in his apartment on Commonwealth Avenue. He cooked his own meals and did his own cleaning, sweeping his floors, dusting his books, emptying his ashtrays. But after six months he was tired and could stand it no longer. Angry at himself for wasting so much time, he looked for a way to escape his situation while avoiding entanglements with women, for he had told himself that no woman would ever again make him suffer, that he would never again follow the siren's song. There was even danger in having a housekeeper. She might be beautiful, and he was defenseless against beauty.

It was an issue of the *Exchange*, bought by chance at a newsstand, which suggested a practical solution to his problem. A "middle-aged colored woman" who could do his chores for several hours a day, was just what he wanted. She was forty or fifty years old, no doubt (as usual, his imagination had begun to work), strong and plump with thick features set in a face as round as the full moon, and she lurched heavily from side to side when she walked. She said "yassuh" and "I does," and her sagging flesh shook with her loud laughter. He was not prejudiced against black people; they were merely men and women of a darker color and he respected them as he respected anyone else. But he had always seen them from afar. He had no Negro acquaintance and could not imagine ever being on intimate terms with a black man or woman. Furthermore, with the woman in question it was certain that the usual problem would not arise.

XXX

"Is this Mrs. Lewis' residence?"

"Yes, it is," said Fanny. She had been waiting all morning for this visit.

"Please tell your mother that the person who wrote concerning a position wishes to speak to her," Donat Sylvain said. He looked closely at the young woman as he entered at her invitation and sat down. She was lithe and slender, her skin was as smooth as silk.

"My mother," thought Fanny, amused; but he was not the first. "I don't have a mother," she said. "I'm . . ."

"Your sister, then?"

"Sir, my sister lives far from here. I know who you're looking for; it's me: I'm Mrs. Lewis." She was expecting a good-humored greeting but instead she saw a look of incredulity on his face.

"How can that be? A 'middle-aged' woman . . ."

"It's me. Believe me. I'm thirty-six; isn't that enough? The magazine that you found my advertisement in is my son's."

Donat Sylvain examined her, not yet convinced. His preconceptions were quickly collapsing. "Truthfully, madam, one wouldn't have believed it," he said, embarrassed, faltering before this unexpected situation. But, after all, he thought, what difference could it make? "Then you know why I am here," he added. "Can you really keep house?"

"It's a job that I'm familiar with," said Fanny,

laughing. "I'm fairly sure I can manage it with no difficulty."

The clear flow of her laughter struck Donat Sylvain. He had never heard anything like it. But that was of little importance. "How many hours a day do you expect to work?"

"Four. Five. It depends. But the work will be well done."

Still uncertain, Donat Sylvain looked vaguely for a way to extricate himself. "You should know," he said, "that I work at home and can't be disturbed. You must'nt make any noise coming and going. And I'm gruff; I have many unpleasant ways. I could be sharp with you sometimes without meaning to be."

"Never mind that," said Fanny, "I'm as quiet as a mouse. And if you were as bad as you say, you wouldn't be aware of it. Let me try for a week. At the end, we'll know each other better. If you're satisfied, then pay me . . . as much as you can."

She was forcing him to make a decision. "Agreed," he said with resignation "Come tomorrow, if that's all right."

When Donat Sylvain had gone, Fanny went back to Irene's apartment. "I have the job! I have the job!" she cried. "But it's going to be difficult. He's not very sociable nor very easy to get along with. I can't move around or make noise. It disturbs him when he's working, he says. As long as he stays out of my way . . ."

"Is he young or old?" asked Irene.

"He's young and nice-looking. But that's the least of my concerns, you know."

"Hm!" said Irene. "Things do happen."

XXXI

Fanny's sons were displeased when she told them of her new job. "Mama," said Frank, "you should have talked to me first. I am able to take care of you by myself. It isn't hard at all." Edward added: "A little patience would have seen things straightened out. I know you blame me for leaving the postal service, but you'll see that I was right."

"Four hours a day is nothing," said Fanny. "We'll be living the same life as before. I'll fix your meals, and Maude Olliver will come during the day to watch the fire so that the house will stay warm."

When she had asked this favor of Maude, she had said to her: "Finish your story. I'm going to be away a lot now, and I've wondered what could have happened to bring you here."

Maude took a deep breath. "The end of my story is one of those turns of the wheel that change the whole course of your life. After four happy years, a letter arrived from the Antilles for Dessie during a time that we were docked in New York. One of his uncles had just died and left him a small plantation near the village where he was born. I could see that it gave Dessie something to think about. That night he came to me and said, 'I was expecting it. I've always told myself that one day I would go back to Bequia and live quietly. It doesn't make any sense to break your back the way we do. I've got savings, and you can live there for next to nothing. You have to work, but you feel free. I'm going to give up the barge and we'll

116

go back there. What do you say?'

"I was jolted by the news. From what he had told me, Bequia was a little no-account island, one of the three hundred strewn about the Caribbean. It's farther away than Havana or Jamaica, near the coast of Venezuela! I wouldn't have minded taking a trip there, but I didn't want to spend the rest of my life stuck in a place like that. I was horrified at the thought, and I told him so. 'It just takes getting used to,' he said. 'It's a question of living like the people there live.' My friends warned me not to be fool enough to go lose myself on that rock. They tried to tell me how different the life there was from ours. They said I wouldn't be able to tolerate it. But I loved my husband, and I made up my mind to follow him wherever he went, whether I liked it or not.

"So, he quit his barge and arranged everything, and two weeks later we booked passage on a steamer that was heading for the Guianas with a stopover at Grenada, nine days' passage in stormy weather at that. From Grenada a second ship carried us to another island named Carriacou, then to another one where we had to charter a small sailboat for the rest of the trip. After thirteen full days, with the hot sun reflecting off the sea right into our faces, we came to Bequia.

"From a distance it was lovely to look at, full of palm trees and banana trees, but it was small! You could take it all in at a glance. There was a green mountain at the center with slopes that ran down to the beach, and nothing else. You could circle the whole island in ten hours. No sign of a river, no spring; nothing but some salt-water wells. They trap rain water in cisterns, in tubs, in whatever is available. And you've never seen such rain. It lasts for months; though, afterwards, you go months without a drop.

117

There's only one village, situated on a large bay; the rest is plantations and scattered huts. I didn't know all that when we landed, but I could see that it wasn't New York or New Bedford. Anyhow, there I was; I had agreed, and Dessie was with me.

"His mother was happy to see us. She was an old black woman, coal-black, so black I was afraid to look at her. We stayed with her until we could get a house. There were no floors and no beds; we slept on mats on the bare ground. I found out right away how they lived. Everybody works in the fields growing sweet potatoes and ground nuts and sugar cane; they pick bananas and cassava and big balls of breadfruit. Men and women get together whenever they feel like it. More marriages take place in the bushes than in church. Besides, it's understood that the young girls can have all the fun they want. But when they're married, it stops. What is really peculiar are the zombies. They work at night and disappear at day-break."

"They disappear? Why?" asked Fanny.

"Why? They're dead people. Every morning they return to their graves in the cemetery."

"Dead people! Maude, don't tell me you saw any of those zombies."

"I didn't see any myself. I didn't go to the fields. But everybody there has seen them. The sorcerers take them from their tombs and put them to work. Only they keep to themselves and don't speak to anybody. Maybe it's just superstition. Those people believe in all kinds of magic. Deeper into the mountain there are obi temples where they practise terrible rites"

"Heavens," said Fanny. "You must have felt safe."

118

"To tell the truth, it didn't make any difference, Mrs. Lewis. I helped the old woman tend her garden and weave mats. I was getting used to it. But a terrible fate awaited me. I noticed that Dessie was neglecting me. The same man who had been so kind and attentive didn't care about me any more. He ordered me around roughly and left me by myself all the time, and I heard it said that he was chasing one girl after another. When I said something, he answered back 'We're not in the United States now.' Well, that wouldn't do. I couldn't sleep. I tried to think of some way to fight back. One night, I was fed up. I caused a violent scene. Without a word he knocked me down, and before I could get up, he began to beat me and kick me. Then he left and I didn't see him again for two days. It was over then. Despite my pleas and his mother's objections, I couldn't count on him for anything, and he beat me at every turn. There they think they can do whatever they want with their women. In less than six months, he had lost all notion of honesty and consideration He had become a 'native,' a half-savage like those around him. How a man could change so fast and so completely is a mystery that I have never understood. It still frightens me when I think about it. I knew two different men. When I think of Dessie, it's either one or the other that comes to me. I can't put them together."

"I understand. What an ordeal it must have been. How did it end?" said Fanny.

"Things went from bad to worse. The kind of life I was leading was intolerable. So I said to my husband, 'You don't love me any more. Send me back to the United States. We'll both be happier.' But, no, he wanted to keep me as his slave. 'It costs too much,' he said. 'When the time comes, I'll see.' Times came

119

and went, but he did nothing. Finally, one night after an argument, after having dragged me out of the hut and having given me a proper beating, he threw me against a large, thorny cactus. I think every needle struck me at the same time. But I had hidden a long knife in my shirt and when he turned his back to me, I threw it at his head. It came to rest in a tree trunk an inch from his ear. Then I said 'You listen to me. If we stay together much longer, one of us is going to get the rope, because either I'll kill you or you'll kill me. Decide. You've beaten me for the last time.' He just sneered. But the English schoolteacher, who was passing by, had seen everything. He came over and said to Dessie, 'This had better stop, boy. Everyone knows how you treat her. If you don't promise to send her back home, I'll go to the mayor and have you arrested.' Dessie was afraid, so he made up his mind. I traveled back the same way I had come and landed in New York with a dollar in my pocket.''

''What a story!'' said Fanny. ''Have you heard anything since?''

''In the whole six years, missus, he hasn't given the least sign of life to his brother or me. I tried to find out if he was dead or alive. I learned recently that he's still on the island and that he's got four children by four different girls. I knew one of them — his stepsister. He'll never come back here. Not that I care, God knows, but every day I ask myself how the man I married could turn into such a brute. And I remind myself that no man will ever get me to believe in him again.''

XXXII

Fanny left for work the next day. Donat Sylvain greeted her politely and told her briefly what he expected of her. Though not rich, the apartment was nicely furnished; Fanny was pleased by the tapestries, water colors and statuettes which decorated its rooms. Between the study which overlooked the avenue and the narrow kitchen there were two rooms: a bedroom, and a living-room which contained a piano, a couch and three chairs.

"That's all of it, madam," said Donat Sylvain. "It has been neglected, so, to begin, it will require a little effort. You will notice," he added, "that my study is situated off from the rest. It isn't necessary to go through it to get to the other rooms. To clean it you will want to choose a time when I am away."

"What do you do about meals?" asked Fanny.

"I fix myself coffee in the mornings. I go out for my other meals. I am used to that system. I will leave you now and return around two o'clock. The house is in your hands."

"Very well, sir. By the time you get back, things will have improved." She bowed slightly, after the fashion of the South, but it seemed to displease him, for he turned and left without another word. "How disagreeable," Fanny thought. "And was it necessary to slam the door?"

She began with the study. Books lined the walls. She was unfamiliar with most of them, but she found several which had been on Mr. Lewis' shelves. There was an unfinished pastel portrait on an easel. On the large table at the center of the room pencils, rulers and rough sketches were scattered about, and there was a composition representing a nymph, her hair blown by the wind, standing on a floating shell. There were all kinds of newspapers and other papers lying about. Admiring his drawings, Fanny remarked to herself that there was at least one thing he knew how to do. But she did not touch the table. She carefully cleaned the rest of the study and then went to the bedroom.

She knew right away that a woman had once lived here. There were still bottles of perfume and powder boxes sitting on top of the dresser. Above the marble-topped dresser there was a portrait of a beautiful young woman, and there were photographs of her on the console tables. Perhaps he was gruff, Fanny thought, but not with everybody. And it was his business.

She was still busy when Donat Sylvain returned. "I didn't touch your papers," she said. "I didn't want to annoy you the first day."

He could not help smiling. "Don't worry," he said," I'll tell you what makes me angry. Everything else seems very clean. That's fine for today."

During the remainder of the week she saw Donat Sylvain for only a few minutes at a time. He stayed in his study with the door closed, ignoring her. On Saturday she knocked at his door.

"Excuse me, sir," she said, "but I think it's time for me to know whether you are satisfied with my work or not."

Donat Sylvain looked at her, and again he was struck by her youthfulness. It was the only thing with which he was not satisfied, for in the past week she had brought him comfort that he had not known for a

122

long time.

"Certainly. You have saved me a great deal of trouble. However, there's one detail. I have heard you singing sometimes. It isn't that I don't like it. You have a very pretty voice. But it distracts me from my work. So, you see . . ."

"As you like. I won't sing any more; that is, if you want me to come again on Monday."

"Of course, of course. Here are your first week's wages. Have you found me tolerable?"

"Better than that. I haven't even seen you. I enjoyed your sketches. I think you're a real artist."

After her departure, Donat Sylvain asked himself what she understood about art. It was true that she seemed intelligent; she must have gone to school. Also, she seemed alert and aware. He wondered if perhaps he had made a mistake in hiring her so quickly. "A middle aged colored woman" indeed! he thought.

At the same time, her employer was on Fanny's mind. It was a shame, she thought, that he was so surly. He must have been hurt by life not to want her even to hum. But he had paid her generously, and in order to live — it might as well be said — a person has to put up with a lot.

XXXIII

Another week passed, and everyone was adapting to the new way of life. Edward and Frank lacked nothing. Their mother was home at the beginning and end of the day, Maude was there in between. Despite her fatigue, Fanny did not complain. She even seemed interested in her second job. "He's a white man," she said to Maude. "He's not very pleasant, but he doesn't annoy you. His motto is: 'Don't bother me, and I won't bother you.'"

It was true that more and more Donat Sylvain seemed to be avoiding Fanny. He said little to her and when they encountered each other, he passed by rudely as though he had something against her. Thus, she was surprised when he opened the forbidden door and invited her into his study.

"Miss, Mrs.," he said hesitantly, "I owe you an apology, and I have a favor to ask of you."

"An apology? Why?" asked Fanny. "I can't imagine . . ."

"Yes. It was rude of me the other day to ask you not to sing. I regretted it right after. I thought your voice had disturbed me, but, on the contrary, when I no longer heard it I realized that I missed it. There's life and joy in your voice. Instead of blocking my pencils, it stimulated them. Please excuse me and sing your beautiful songs again."

"If that's what it was, why, you had every right. I'm surprised that my songs please you. I just sing

124

without thinking about it.''

"Yes, but you make others think. Tell me, where did you learn?''

"Oh, in the South in a church choir, and rocking my children.''

Pensively, Donat Sylvain said: ''Your voice is extraordinary. It has the quality of a fine steel blade. When you sing 'Swing low, sweet chariot' it's enough to bring tears to one's eyes.''

"Ah, well, I won't sing that any more. It seems to me that you don't need anyone around making you cry.''

Their eyes met, and Donat Sylvain wondered if this young woman had guessed his sorrow. ''Sing it anyway,'' he said. ''And after, to make me happy, sing that 'tick-tock, tick-tock.' '' Then, for the first time, he laughed in her presence.

Fanny left the room, touched by the words of the man who she had believed paid no attention to her. From then on she sang whenever she wished, singing no longer for herself alone but, for the listener on the other side of the wall as well; and Donat Sylvain greeted her always with a friendly word and a smile.

XXXIV

"What I would like," said Fanny, "is a dark blue or black one-piece dress that hangs very straight, and a white apron, long, that attaches to the shoulders, with a thin lace border."

"Here is the perfect uniform for housekeeping, madam," the clerk said. "And here is a cap that goes well with it. It also keeps the dust out of your hair."

Fanny felt the fabric. "Fine. I'll take it. Please wrap it for me," she said. Until then she had worn her ordinary clothes to work at Donat Sylvain's apartment, but of late she had begun to feel slovenly in them. When she returned home, she tried on her new uniform. She laughed when she saw herself in the mirror. "Perhaps he won't like it," she thought. But she put her mind at ease, deciding that, after all, it was for her own pleasure.

When Donat Sylvain opened the door to greet her, he was astonished by what he saw. "I didn't recognize you," he said. "My compliments. You make a very attractive housekeeper."

For the first time he looked at her with an artist's eye, and noticed her slim graceful figure in that sober dress. The apron's cut brought her full, round bust and the fine proportions of her head into relief. Her arms emerged from her short sleeves like two firm, supple stalks. There was an exquisite harmony of colors in her brown skin, the discreet blue of her dress and the immaculate white of her apron.

"You see, I was the only thing left in your house that looked neglected, sir. And I open the door for your clients and for salesmen sometimes."

"It's fine," Donat Sylvain said, "though it wasn't necessary. I shall pretend that I have another Tanagra."

"What is a Tanagra, sir?"

"A statue of a brown-skinned woman. Like the one on the piano here."

"You're mistaken, Mister Sylvain, if you think I'm a statue," said Fanny to herself.

Some days later, in Donat Sylvain's absence, while she was dusting his study, she lifted a book and a paper slid from beneath it onto the floor. She picked it up, but as she was about to replace it, she stopped suddenly, shocked. The paper contained a carefully drawn sketch in three colors. Fanny recognized the bronze-colored woman dressed in rich blue and brilliant white as herself. Donat Sylvain had replaced the cap with a band of ribbon and the apron had become a kind of loose-hanging drapery. She contemplated the drawing for several minutes, amazed that he had made such an effort as the lines seemed to suggest. Donat Sylvain, then, was less aloof than she thought. She attributed his secretiveness to prejudice. He was aware of her but he did not want her to know it. "Perhaps if I were white," Fanny thought, "he wouldn't be ashamed." This notion lingered in her mind. For the first time in her life she regretted the fate that had deprived her of the privileges of others. "If I were white," she continued, "he would say, 'I think you're very nice looking. I've drawn your portrait. Here it is.' " She could not allow herself to dream further.

XXXV

Another time Donat Sylvain came home early to find Fanny seated in his armchair absorbed in reading one of his books. The scene should have displeased him, but instead he felt a keen sorrow. The image of the woman he had loved came sharply back to him. He had so often seen her in the same chair, seated in exactly the same way. He remembered her beauty, her frivolous laughter; now she was gone. He was unable to say why finding another woman in her place did not offend him. She, too, was young and, in a different way, charming. At that moment the two women's faces merged into an indistinct shadow of love missed, of a companion asked for in vain, whom he no longer had nor would ever have.

Startled, Fanny leapt quickly to her feet. "Please excuse me, Mr. Sylvain," she said. "I know I was wasting time, but my cleaning is finished."

"What were you reading?" asked Donat Sylvain softly.

"*Evangeline*. We had to read extracts in school, but I never read it through."

"It deserves to be read. There's nothing wrong with it. In fact, you seem to have had a good education."

"No. But we had a very capable schoolteacher. He loved poetry: Scott, Bryant, Whittier, all of them."

"What interests you most in *Evangeline*?"

"The story itself. The two lovers parted by fate. It seems so pitiful."

"Yes, and much less rare than we think. Do you

know," he continued after a short silence, "that a moment ago you reminded me of just such a story?"

"I don't know how, sir, but it doesn't surprise me. Everything reminds us of what we regret, and it's clear that something is grieving you."

"You think so, do you? Please tell me what gives you that idea."

"There are signs. First, you're not happy. You never make jokes. I don't mean with me, of course, but with your visitors. You haven't gone to the theater once in two months. You're too serious for a man your age. And those photographs in your bedroom, all of the same person; they're not there for nothing. Every time I straighten them, I come back to find them moved. You don't leave them alone."

Donat Sylvain lowered his head guiltily as though he had been caught at some wrong-doing. "What you say is true. But there's nothing one can do, is there?"

I'm not so sure, sir. You could at least not be a stranger in your own house. All you have here is a study. You never touch the piano, you never wear slippers. And I wonder why you eat out. It would be simple for me to fix you a meal. If there's no hope that your friend will come back . . ."

"Yes? What remedy do you have for that?"

"Well, don't keep the perfume bottles and the bits of lace that she left lying around. Those things break your heart. Just keep the portrait, not the photographs; it's too easy for you to pick them up and kiss them."

"I think you're a bit of a witch," said Donat Sylvain, laughing in spite of himself and thinking that nothing seemed to escape this brown woman's attention. Why not, he continued silently, try her remedy? "Suppose I let you arrange my room exactly as you see fit?"

"Oh, I wouldn't want to, it's none of my business. I just said what came into my mind. But, for the rest, I think you should consider them."

The next day Fanny was surprised to see that all of the phials and lace had disappeared from Donat Sylvain's bedroom. Alone on the wall was the portrait in the large frame, as seductive as ever but inaccessible to kisses.

In turn, that same evening Donat Sylvain got a surprise. Just as he was leaving for dinner, Fanny opened the livingroom door and he saw that the table was set and covered with a white tablecloth. In the center of a plate garnished with egg-plant sat a steaming chicken.

XXXVI

Their relationship was changing subtly. To Donat Sylvain, Fanny had become more than a simple domestic. She was an aide, almost a friend, and the loneliness of the past months had disappeared. He sensed her sincerity and devotion, and each day he found qualities in her which pleased him. Instead of shunning her, he was happy to have her with him, and the rooms seemed empty when she was gone.

He now allowed her to read in his study, even when he was working there himself. "Provided that you be quiet," he told her. But it was he who disturbed her. "You're good at spelling," he would say, "tell me how to spell 'the breadth of a dreadnought.' There are

130

words in English that trip me up every time." Or: "How many stars do I put on the American flag?" Fanny would quickly call Mr. Lewis' lessons to mind and give him the answer. He demanded that she sit at the table with him during meals. "Don't think," he said, "that color makes any difference in my opinion of people. I see color solely in physical terms. I don't like any color that is impure, banal, without character. It's as simple as that. And there are many brown things which are beautiful." To himself he added, "such as you."

One day he heard her singing the lyric, "Drink to me only with thine eyes." Her voice, as light and clear as ever, carried him to the piano which had remained untouched for several months, and he provided accompaniment for the sad melody. From time to time after that, he would ask her to sing a spiritual or a song that had pleased him, such as "Grandfather's Clock." But she refused to sing "Swing low, sweet chariot." "You're mournful enough as it is," she said.

With Maude's help, she continued to give her sons all that they needed and somehow she found time to address copies of the *Exchange*. Her friends thought that she was happier since she had begun to work. "Your Frenchman," Irene asked, "is he tamer?" "He's still moody," Fanny answered, "but I can take it."

In truth, Fanny was happier. She was enchanted. She knew quite well that Donat Sylvain found her attractive and that he was interested in her. She was attracted by him, too. She could not hide from herself the tender desire that she felt towards him, and she wondered whether this time she might find love as someone's equal and not as a submissive student;

131

love freely given by a man her own age who owed her nothing. Would she be loved by a white man, she wondered, just as her grandmother had been, but this time not as a slave? She could not rid her mind of this beautiful dream. She was still the audacious, restless Fanny who had fought and beaten Charlie Ross and thrown pillows at Mr. Lewis. "It will take more than tossing a few pillows at him," she reflected. "But he likes me, brown as I am. And he likes my voice, and that is something!"

XXXVII

Both Fanny and Donat Sylvain felt themselves to be in an awkward situation; they were close together and distant from each other at the same time. But one evening Fanny was unusually nervous, she sought some way for them to break out of their mutual embarrassment.

"Why do you always call me Mrs. Lewis," she asked suddenly. "I'm your servant, so call me Fanny. Maids and housekeepers are called by their first names."

"Is your name Fanny?" asked Donat Sylvain. "I didn't know. Well, listen, I'll call you Fanny, but for another reason: because you're not my servant."

"Please tell me what you mean."

"You are a lovely, warm-hearted woman who has helped me and done me a lot of good. 'Servant' is a word that means nothing at all to me. I consider you ny equal. Say that we're a team. You do one half of he work and I do the other.''

"You're very kind, Mr. Sylvain. So we're, as you say, partners?''

"That's right. We will struggle against fate toge-her.''

Out of timidity and because of his almost mystical espect for women, up to now he had refrained from expressing his real feelings for Fanny, but he was about to overcome his fear, for he clearly saw that his young daughter of Africa differed greatly from the other women he had known. He felt secure in her ands. She was not fickle; she would not betray him. he gave him faith in true love. Silent for the moment, e spoke with his eyes. Fanny saw them become moist.

"You know,'' she said, "for partners we're playing peculiar game. We hide our cards from each other; 'e're not following suit.''

"Explain that to me, Fanny.''

"Here it is. I'll say what I think. I think that you ve me enough, anyway And I love you dearly.''

What followed was what their destiny dictated. onat Sylvain was neither surprised nor overwhelm-1. He approached Fanny silently and put his arms ound her.

XXXVIII

It was a strange bond between two different but equally passionate people. Donat Sylvain's love was like an even, intense flame, while Fanny's was like series of brilliant flashes. Both had been imprisoned by life, both had given themselves to others only to receive nothing in return, and both were eager for a totally absorbing and complete relationship. They needed no preamble or explanations. From the start there was a perfect, unspoken accord between them.

"Do you want me to put her portrait away?" Donat Sylvain asked.

"No," said Fanny, "leave it out; memories have their place. I'll make sure that it doesn't hurt you."

She did not show him the humble deference that she had shown Mr. Lewis. She was his companion and confident counselor; she gave advice and made decisions, finding at last in Donat Sylvain someone who treated her opinions with respect. She devoted herself entirely to her new-found love. She stayed with him as long as she could every day, going happily back and forth between the two apartments. No one suspected her secret. When Irene or Maude questioned her about her employer, she would reply: "Don't speak of him, I think he's getting worse." But her sons had noticed a change in her. "You're getting younger every minute, mama," they said. For Fanny had returned to the springtime of her youth with the love she had sought all her life, a love freely given and received.

She gave her "white man" the passion he had missed.
It brought Donat Sylvain back to life; he accepted it
humbly and gratefully, standing bewitched as she
danced before him (she was not embarrassed now),
or when she sang.

My grandfather said of those he could hire,
Not a servant so faithful he found;
For it wasted no time and had but one desire —
At the close of each week to be wound.
And it kept in its place — not a frown on its face,
And its hands never hung by its side;
But it stopped short — never to go again —
When the old man died.

Ninety years without slumbering (tick-tock, tick-
tock),
His life seconds numbering (tick-tock, tick-tock).

He asked her to tell him of her life. He was touched
by the story of her youth in Greenway and of her mar-
iage to Mr. Lewis; he, too, was possessed of a guile-
ess, primitive nature. He envied Charlie Ross who had
played and fought with her. He would have liked to
ee her grow up with her children; she had been at
once big sister and mother to them. He became in-
erested in films and concerts again, and they went to
hem often. In the beginning they would leave his
partment separately at intervals of several minutes
nd meet at the theater where as if by chance they
ound themselves seated next to one another. "You
an't allow yourself to be seen in my company," she
aid. But he grew tired of subterfuge, seeing it as
owardice, and soon without affectation or bravado
hey were walking together on the street and sitting
ogether on buses and in restaurants. "I don't care

what some imbeciles think. When we go out, I want you to be with me,'' he told her. Occasionally, some young man or a huffy dowager would stare at them but most of the time they passed unnoticed. In general the American deserves his reputation as someone who minds his own business.

One evening they went to one of the few dance halls where the two races were admitted. Donat Sylvain wanted to see some signs of the growing decline of prejudice. The crowd had a respectable, middle-class appearance. Black, white and mixed couples were dancing together and the hall was orderly. "Dance with all the white girls you want," said Fanny, "but if you look at a single black girl, I'll be very jealous."

Another time, when they were in Roxbury they were attracted by shouts and a confusion of noises coming from a basement. Written in chalk on one of the basement's windows were the words: "Church of God Salvation through the blood of Christ.''

"Well, it's not a cathedral," said Donat Sylvain "Could there still be catacombs down there? Let's go in and see."

They found themselves in a narrow, poorly-lit room filled with wooden chairs. Some thirty people were gathered there, men and women of various ages with their children. They clapped their hands as they sang a spiritual to the accompaniment of a temperamental harmonium. On a raised platform at the far end a black woman was walking back and forth singing with the others, as she clapped out the lively rhythm. There was little doubt that she was the singular chapel's minister. In spite of the general fervor, heads had turned at the sound of the door opening and thirty pairs of eyes looked questioningly at the newcomers. Embarrassed, Fanny and Donat Sylvain had taken seats
136

he rear, hoping to be forgotten. But their presence, Donat Sylvain's especially, was a rare event. When he hymn was over, the woman preacher read verses from the Bible. Then she said: "Brothers and sisters, before going any further, maybe our new brother would like to testify." "Amen," said a chorus of voices. Donat Sylvain's first impulse was to flee, but after a few moments he rose and walked down the aisle to the platform. Then he turned to the assembly and spoke. He told them how much he admired their mystical ardor. He told them that he prayed to Christ with them to reward their faith. They were the little flock which had been promised preference over the proud multitudes. In spirit, he said, he was one of them. He would carry a memory of this meeting which would comfort him always, and he would have more esteem than ever for their pious and faithful race. As the applause sounded, a new hymn was begun. This time Fanny sang, too; as clear as an angel's, her voice soared high above the others.

When they were in the street, Fanny said: "Dear Donat, you got out of that well."

"Why not," Donat Sylvain replied. "I was serious. Everything that I said came from my heart."

XXXIX

Fanny would have been content, but for her sons. George remained with Celia. Fanny knew that they argued and that the girl, leading her usual life, treated him shabbily. George visited her now and then but when she spoke to him of Celia, he refused to listen. "She's got the devil in her," he admitted, "but I love her anyway." Her son's infatuation troubled her. She did not consider that her own heart had known instances of such blind loyalty.

Moreover, Edward was having difficulties again. His failures still depressed her, but she was no longer surprised by them. She had come to regard her eldest son as a child who would never grow up and who would be dependent on her his whole life. She considered it her duty to care for him and to keep him amused. He was as gay and carefree as ever; one illusion replaced another in his mind with ease. "He wants for nothing," Fanny said to herself, "because he only needs dreams."

Following in the footsteps of its predecessor, the *Universal Exchange* had come to nothing. Its numbers appeared infrequently despite the stacks of correspondence filling the drawers, for the correspondence consisted largely of appeals from women, which he had offered to print free of charge. Most of the copies sent to newsstands were returned to him. Edward consoled himself, saying that he owed nothing to anyone, but, of course, he was mistaken. He had not finished

138

paying for his equipment. He sacrificed many pieces
in order to save others, but finally he was left with
a tiny pedal press on which, composing all of the pages
alone, he printed a smaller version of his magazine.
His basement was almost empty. He thought hard of
a way to make the best of his situation.

"Mama," he said, "I know that I haven't yet had
any success, but this time I've learned my lesson.
What I've been missing till now was simply capital.
I've learned that capital is the indispensable lever in
any human effort. It isn't fair, I know, because the
essence of any enterprise should be talent. But I need
a business that doesn't demand capital, where I can
start with nothing and finally produce something. If
it exists, I'll find it, don't worry."

A short time later, Edward thought that he had found
it. He took to the streets of Boston with a hand-cart.
He went into alleyways and backyards, digging in
garbage cans; he collected wood from demolished
buildings and coal which had fallen from overloaded
trucks and offered to relieve housewives of their
rubbish. He returned to his basement with heaps of
cast-off objects: suits, furniture, paper, metal, which
he would pick through and separate immediately. His
mother tried to dissuade him from this activity, but
he replied: "It's the only business that functions without capital. My stock costs me nothing. What I don't
throw away, I sell to wholesale junk dealers. It's clear
profit for me. I'm not put out or humiliated by my
trade. One kind of labor is as good as another. Plus,
the fresh air is good for me, and I have time to write.
Here, mama," he said, kissing his mother, "take
the first dollar I've earned." She was proud of her
son. At least he was courageous and did not yield
easily when confronted with adversity. She could be

139

pleased that he had a job that was not too taxing. There were no responsibilities or risks, and the work was sufficient to his needs, perhaps, and allowed him time for his whims. At this point, he could only improve himself. She was surprised when, one Sunday, he appeared before her in a new suit bought with money that he had earned.

The *Exchange*'s 'office' was in complete disorder. His press, type and desk had been pushed into an obscure corner by his collections; the rest of the space was seemingly given over to a pile of junk thrown together as by a cyclone. The basement's only window was cluttered with notices and signs of the two businesses: "The director of the *Exchange* will be absent each day except for Saturday from nine o'clock A.M. to three o'clock P.M.;" "A selection of repaired shoes now on sale;" "Poets: please leave your contributions in the box;" "Children invited to collect old newspapers, for which we pay cash;" "Meetings of the Literary Club are held each Thursday evening. Enter by the back door."

XI

Fanny did not speak of her family's problems to Donat Sylvain. She wanted their life together to remain free of the complications of Roxbury. They were the classic lovers who forgot the world around them in each other's presence. The effect of their long delay in expressing their love was to sharpen and intensify desire. Their caresses were like those of impassioned honeymooners.

Playful as ever, Fanny took delight in teasing her lover. He would return to find her lying on the carpet, perhaps scantily dressed and with her arms folded in the pose of a sacrificial victim, or to be greeted with the sensual gestures of an oriental dancer. At other times, for no reason she would fling herself imploringly at his knees. They laughed together at her childishness. She would pretend to be jealous, accusing him of infidelity, then she would throw her arms around his neck, saying, "You know that you can do as you like." But, out of fear, she never mentioned the woman in the portrait.

Donat Sylvain was a poet and it was his pleasure when they were alone to construct fantasies around Fanny. She was, he claimed, a distant cousin of the Shulamite of whom Solomon had sung. Her body was a precious jewel-box of mirages and symbols. The color of her skin reflected golden bees, rare orchids, polished wood, ripe chestnuts, fine topaz, delicate coffee, the shimmering brilliance of insects' wings, the down on the breasts of birds. In her perfect limbs was the suppleness of young palms, the agile grace of gazelles. The harmony of her movements held the measure of swaying boughs. Her voice carried the echo of cords vibrating in the breeze. The earthly Fanny laughed at his lyrical musings, but in spite of herself she was proud of the dignity and majesty which he attributed to her. Happy to be elevated into a world created especially for her, she accepted her role as idol, giving gifts to her neophyte which were worthy of a goddess.

To his mind, she presented perplexing problems as well. At times, listening to reason, he saw her as his sister, separated by negligible differences. For what were the differences which divided the races? Less than those which divided many other kinds of groups. What nonsense it was to allow these differences to prevent human fraternity and unity. Daughters of Japhet or daughters of Ham — the mold was the same; it was the heart and soul which counted. Fanny was as intelligent and as gracious and beautiful as any woman among the blonde Nordic elite. Why should she be subservient to them? In the face of stupid prejudice he found justice in honoring and praising her. Upon rendering her some humble service, he liked to say to her, "It is an apology to all of your race." For him she was simply a woman, distinguished solely by the rare qualities that he would have admired in a person of any color. No woman of another race could have been closer to him.

But at other moments she seemed a creature from far away who differed greatly from himself, someone whom it would have taken a miracle to understand. How could he be sure that the two races had known common origins, and should share the same name? He recalled the legend of a black Adam unknown to the other, who perhaps had been born of a germ which came from another planet. Was the reflection in her eye a spark from an unknown star? Her voice had an unearthly tone. At these moments she was surrounded by the halo of a houri fallen from an astral paradise. She became a supernatural nymph taking her sport in the land of men, and his attraction for her then was an aberrant force futilely seeking to unite two beings of alien essences. He would caress her like a man transported, with the almost sacrilegious headiness of one entering forbidden reaches.

He liked, further, to see her as an *enfant sauvage*

fresh from the jungle with the perfume of her virginal nature still about her. He pictured her wandering ancestors of less than two centuries ago, as they made their way through the labyrinthine bush. She, too, would have carried jars down to the large lakes and danced to the furious drums. Her voice would have risen with Dahomian chants or murmured prayers to fetishes. She would have harvested corn in sandy plains. Tigers would have lain in wait and pursued her. In a violent mood, fate had uprooted her and set her down in a strange land which little by little had fashioned her anew. But beneath the finished surface lived the girl of old, naked and burnt by the fires of the sun. Her primitive heart had persisted; it was faithful to its native ground. She was as natural, as self-contained and spontaneous as dawn or a storm. He loved her for it. She had taught him how to live again on his own original soil.

Quite simply, the meaning of these rambling thoughts was that he loved her, and like a lover he was embellishing his love with splendid ornament.

XLI

"Mama," said Frank one evening, "guess who I met on the street."

"There are so many people on the street," said Fanny.

"Yes, but would you expect to bump into Charlie Ross?"

"Don't tell me that Charlie Ross is in Boston?" said Fanny.

"He just arrived and was looking for us. I would have brought him over right away, but he had to claim his trunk. He's coming to see you tomorrow morning."

"Oh, yes, let him come," said Fanny. "Poor Charlie. He too has come to seek his fortune."

Though she did not understand the reason, her son's news had unsettled Fanny momentarily. But she was quite willing to see Charlie. He was kind; he felt no ill-will towards her for her rebuffs, and he was always ready to help her. She was ready in turn to help him if she could.

"You weren't expecting me, were you Fanny?" said Charlie Ross the next day, after she had served him lunch. "But I had enough of cotton and the woods. Greenway is more dead than ever. Not one of our old friends is left, now. Nicky was the last to leave. Do you remember him? He's the one who made us laugh so much. I told myself, 'I'm getting out of here, too,' and you know how I am. No sooner said than done."

"Well," said Fanny, "I hope you'll be pleased here. Work is hard to find, but my boys and I can help you out. By the way, she continued, "you must have seen my sister Linda."

"Oh, she sold the house after Mr. Lewis died. She works as a maid now for the Jenkins family. I told her I was leaving. She didn't seem to think much of the idea. You know how old maids are. And you, Fanny, I swear you haven't aged a bit. You've got a nice place here. I can see you're doing well. Frank told me you've got a spare room. Would you mind putting me up for a few days? I'll pay you, don't worry, I just need a little time to get settled."

144

"I wouldn't refuse you, Charlie, You've always been good to me. I hope now that you're a man you've calmed down some?"

"Me? I don't know. I'm just the way I've always been, except that I only get drunk on holidays now."

"You're making progress; and it so happens that the Fourth of July won't be here for six months."

"Well, thank you, Fanny, I'll make it up to you. Come and tell me where to put my clothes."

XLII

Charlie Ross soon discovered that it would take more time than he had thought for him to "get settled." He left every morning to search for a job, but after a few hours he returned disgusted, without success. "Boston is more dead than Greenway," he said. Meanwhile, he helped Fanny to polish her furniture and to do her washing. "I don't like to see you wear yourself out when you come home from work," he said. "Who do you work for?"

"I'm a housekeeper," Fanny replied evasively.

"When I begin to make some money, you won't have to wait on anybody," Charlie Ross said. "You'll be able to tend your own house. You know, he added, "I'm glad to be with you. It brings back old times. Do you remember when we used to steal strawberries from old mother Hemingway? We've been through a lot together, haven't we?"

Although Edward and Frank were much younger

than Charlie Ross, they got along well with him and enjoyed his inoffensive gruffness. From time to time they found a half-day's work for him through friends. But, more often, he remained at the apartment in the afternoons alone, save for the times when Maude Olliver came, who, wary of all men as usual, hardly spoke to him. But when Fanny returned, his boredom was ended. Her simple presence made him feel better and put him in a good mood. At night she played cards with him and her two boys, and he insisted that Fanny play opposite him. 'She's my old partner,' he'd say. "Without her I wouldn't have a bit of luck." The word 'partner' reminded Fanny of the other allegiance she had formed, and for a time she was lost in thought. But Charlie Ross brought her out of it with a loud laugh. "Boys, you don't know what playmates we were, your mama and me, and what a devil she was jumping ditches and fences."

When they were alone, he said coaxingly: "Don't forget that you still have that debt."

"You can cross that off your books, Charlie Ross," she replied. Two kisses, she thought, was not a great deal. But she knew that if she yielded once, there would be no end to it.

"What?" he insisted. "You can't use Mr. Lewis as an excuse now."

"It doesn't matter. I'm taking my revenge for that dirty trick you played on me."

She thought frequently of George and Celia. She no longer saw them, but she received news of them through Charlie Ross, who paid them occasional visits.

XLIII

This was a time when new ideas were making themselves felt among the black people of the United States. The first years after emancipation had found them hopeful of the future. They believed that the South's defeat heralded the decline of prejudice and that from then on they would share in the task of reconstruction with the whites. They consented to social isolation until the time when, by the progress of their race, they would merit equality. "Cooperate with the white man" became the password of Booker T. Washington and other respected black leaders. While waiting for better days, the argument went, make every effort to educate and enrich yourselves.

But black people quickly saw that the other race had no intention of ever dealing with them as equals. There were exceptional cases — white men and women of vision who founded schools of higher education for them, and organized societies to protect their rights — but most of their former masters remained hostile towards them and thought only of keeping them in subjection. They circumvented the laws which made black people citizens, and forced them to submit to insulting segregation while terrorizing them with lynchings and forbidding them access to free economic competition, leaving no way open for them to develop and profit by their talents.

In spite of everything, black people grew conscious of themselves and reacted against this sham alliance.

They were indignant over the fact that they constituted close to ten percent of the nation's population, and yet had practically no influence on its affairs. New leaders who spoke louder and were less pliant arose to denounce the long-time injustices and to call for a struggle to end them. Naturally, they were called "agitators." An agitator is a man who annoys others by asking for what is owed him when it would be simpler to remain quiet. Asa Philip Randolph, Eugene Jones, Walter White, were some of these troublesome champions. They demanded the admission of blacks to labor unions, the participation of blacks in civic affairs; they demanded that blacks be hired by businesses which were supported by blacks. Women were the one part of Afro-America which white men had never scorned, but now black and brown women professed their contempt for white skin, and formed leagues whose members swore never to be touched by it. Organized resistance had replaced humble acquiescence.

Charlie Ross brought with him to Boston the results of this wave of antipathy. He had read Harlem newspapers and had listened as itinerant apostles preached revolt, and his simplistic mind had conceived a rancor bordering on hatred for all white persons without distinction. His experiences with them did nothing to soften his feelings. "They're all alike, North or South," he said. "I beg them for jobs and they say: 'Sorry.' But the day's coming when they won't be able to stop us from living any more." Frank, whose employer treated him kindly, told him that he should not classify all whites together, but he would not listen.

Finally, he found a steady job loading trucks. The crates were heavy and the pace was fast. This was no longer the indolent life of the South. But he was proud to be earning a wage. Each Saturday he paid rent to Fanny, who had agreed to let him live with them. He still tried, unsuccessfully, to become Fanny's lover.

"You're free," he said to her. "Why can't I be closer to you? Don't you get bored all alone?"

"Alone?" she exclaimed. "With three men around me?"

"You know what I mean," he replied. "I never forgot you; I've wanted you all my life."

"Now, now," said Fanny, "enough of that foolishness. Do you see us being lovers after all our battles and escapades? I admit you're my close friend, but anything more would be ridiculous."

She felt cruel to speak in that way, but she had no choice. Besides, she did not fear him. He would always follow her wishes, willingly or not.

XLIV

Above all, Fanny and Donat Sylvain were united in spirit and thought. It had not been long before he saw beneath her apparent frivolity an astonishing young woman of rich, lively intelligence who was capable of grasping the most diverse concepts. She now had the opportunity to demonstrate the knowledge that she had acquired without effort through Mr. Lewis' teaching. Donat Sylvain was amazed to hear her refer casually to points of history or art of which he himself was ignorant. She was especially versed in the poetry and music of her race. She recited to him the poems of Claude

149

McKay, Paul Dunbar, James Johnston and Langston Hughes in which he found a rare, original beauty. "Did you know," she said, "that the great Russian poet Pushkin was the grandson of an Ethiopian prince?" She spoke to him of the melodies of Coleridge Taylor, the operas of Lawrence Freedman, of the singers Roland Hayes, Paul Robeson and Jules Bledsoe. "They're the best," she said, "but we all have music in our blood. Our spirituals were composed by ignorant slaves."

Donat Sylvain could judge the art of Negro comedians and dramatic actors for himself. He and Fanny frequented theaters, and besides going to vaudeville houses, which presented eccentric dancers, jazz singers and blues singers, they saw many plays beautifully performed by black troupes. They admired Charles Gilpin in Eugene O'Neill's *Emperor Jones*; they were moved by the tragic realism of the scenes and the beauty of the choir in *Porgy and Bess*. But the play which made the strongest impression on Donat Sylvain because of its extraordinary inventiveness and superb execution was the *Green Pastures*, a transformation into popular drama of all of biblical history, as naive black people might conceive it.

There were many dangers in the attempt and such subtle, delicate tact was necessary that the success of the actors was a tour de force. The play presented the Eternal Father surrounded by angels and the elect presiding over a fish-fry. In a loft that had little of the Elysian about it, the Lord, seated at an old desk, was taking stock of the way the world was running. Near him, Gabriel came close to sounding the world's end as he brought his trumpet distractedly to his lips. The Creator, dissatisfied with human beings, descended to earth for a personal inspection dressed in a black

150

suit and top hat, distributing expensive cigars. He met some young girls who flirted with him and some bullies who refused to listen to him, and he came upon some kneeling men who he thought were praying but who instead were deeply involved in a dice game. Disgusted, he resolved to destroy the race, so he traced the plan of the ark for Noah with a blue pencil, and debated with him the amount of liquor that should be taken in case of snake bite.

The entire play was set in this vein. The dialogue was full of startling remarks. In sum, it was a parody alongside of which Scarron's *Virgil* seemed heavy and colorless. In the hands of Richard Harrison and his excellent players, the caricature became a touching mystery, intense, reverent and dignified, where tiny cherubim could cling to benign Jehovah's coat-tails, and fat, matronly angels could go about cleaning paradise in stiffly starched aprons, their wings covered to protect them from the dust; where even the Lord could sigh with weariness and say: "Being God isn't always a bed of roses." Nothing about it was scandalous or sacrilegious. There was such profound simplicity, such mystical zeal in every scene that the Old Testament was transfigured and infused with new life. Ministers praised the performances and the show lasted six years, to be interrupted only by the death of the All-Powerful himself.

Donat Sylvain came away from these experiences with increased respect for the mind and the aesthetic sensibilities of black people; counting the achievements bearing their stamp, he concluded that if there was a distinctive American art, it was they who had created it.

XLV

Her work over, Fanny was seated in an armchair in Donat Sylvain's study; Donat Sylvain himself was out on business. She was looking at a book of engravings, but several times she raised her eyes as other thoughts took hold of her. She thought of the happiness which had come to her, of the peace of her days. The green trees of the avenue swaying outside of the window, the yellow sun, the soft breeze blowing over her were symbols of a mood which caused her heart to swell. She moved with the trees, she followed the sunlight and breezes on their journey through space. She had never felt so free and confident. In six months no cloud had come to cast a shadow over her love. Her lover was ever tender and attentive. It was as though an actual vow united them, as though there was no part of life which they did not live together. She still feared his former lover a little. She would stand no chance against such a woman; that was certain. But the woman was gone, never to return, and he could look calmly at her portrait now. She closed her book, and looking about her at the place which she could call her own, she began to sing a lullaby from her childhood.

The doorbell rang and she got up to answer it, asking herself who the unexpected visitor could be. But when she opened the door, she almost fainted.

Standing self-assured before her was a tastefully dressed young woman whose blonde curls fell down around the light skin of her face. Fanny recognized her immediately as the woman in the portrait.

"Does Mister Sylvain still live here?" the woman asked.

"Yes, madam," said. Fanny. "I'm his housekeeper."

"Then tell him, please, that Lucy wishes to speak with him."

"Mister Sylvain is not here at the moment, madam."

"Where is he? Do you know?"

"Downtown on business. But he'll be back in an hour or two."

"Oh, as soon as that?" said Lucy. "I think I'll wait for him. It's all right. I know him very well." She entered the living room and remained standing as she inspected the walls and the furniture. "I think it will be more convenient if I wait for him in his study. It will be a surprise for him." Without further ado she went into the other room and sat down in the wide armchair, first lifting the book which Fanny had left upon it. "That's just like him. Leaving books everywhere. Tell me, have you been working for him long?"

"Nearly eight months," said Fanny, tortured by the conversation.

"Eight months," said Lucy, thinking aloud. "Then six other months. He wasn't expecting me to be gone for so long. I won't keep you," she concluded as she lit a cigarette. "Don't say that I've come. I want to see his face when he finds me here."

Fanny closed the door, crossed the living room unsteadily and slumped into a kitchen chair. Her heart, so alive and happy a few moments ago, felt tortured now. "The other" had returned. His first love had come back to reassume her place. There was no hope of meeting the challenge of one so beautiful and self-assured. When Donat returned and saw her, he was sure to fall in love with her again. One look, one caress, would be sufficient to win him back. Fanny saw them embracing, continuing their interrupted voyage on a small boat which would carry her love away from her forever. She had been nothing but a chapter, a short interlude in a life which had regained its course, leaving her behind, discarded upon the shore. She must refuse any temptation to resist, for the struggle was an impossible one; to set herself up as this woman's rival was absurd pretension. Besides, it would make Donat unhappy, and her love for him could not tolerate the idea. She understood that he would return to this woman who was of his own race and who surpassed both in beauty and mind her poor Southern self. But the thought made her even more despondent.

She remained seated with her hands pressed hard against her temples as the tears ran down her cheeks. She did not know what to do. At length, however, her heart's clear vision replaced her mind's confusion. She decided to yield without struggle and without complaint. All that destiny had brought her was one more sacrifice. What she had done for Mr. Lewis, she would do for Donat Sylvain. First Martha Bledsoe, now Lucy. Why must it always be that those she loved were stolen from her? She would remove herself. She would not be a hindrance. Discussion and explanations were useless. It was best to go away before Donat returned in order to spare him any further shock. If he did not see her again, then it would be easier for him to forget her. Fanny feared, too, that she might cry in front of the woman when she and Donat parted.

She rose to her feet slowly and gathered her few belongings into an overnight bag. Then she straightened and meticulously dusted the furniture for the last time. Lastly, she wrote Donat Sylvain a note which she sealed in an envelope and placed on the table.

"Mr. Sylvain," the note read, "don't be surprised not to see me again. You understand the reason. I have been happy in your service and I thank your for your kindness. Fanny."

She put on her coat and with her bag under her arm she tiptoed out of the door, closing it quietly behind her.

XLVI

Maude was surprised to see Fanny return before the usual hour. "Your work finished so soon today?" she inquired.

"Yes," said Fanny, "and I think it's finished for good. Mister Sylvain ran across an old housekeeper of his that he liked very much, so he's going to rehire her."

"Is that so?" said Maude. "Well, that's too bad. It was a good job. I hope you're not sad."

"Me? Why, no," said Fanny. "That job got on my nerves. I'll get another one soon anyway."

She thanked Maude for having helped her. Then when she was alone she shut herself in her room and gave way to her feelings. It seemed to her that her life had been torn up by its roots. She was weary and despondent, indifferent towards the world, though at moments she shook with rage and said over and over, "I won't accept it! I won't accept it!" But she knew that she had accepted it, that she had again bowed to fate. Her emotions ran their course. Two hours later, exhausted, she was able to consider the life that once again she was being forced to resume. She heard Charlie Ross enter the apartment, so she bathed her eyes and fixed her face. Then her sons returned. Seeing them gave her some solace. Her family was still there to be loved and served. She prepared supper for them, and a short time later Mrs. Lattimore came down for a talk.

"You know," she said to Fanny, "I'm getting worried about Irene. She doesn't do anything halfway, and she's capable of every kind of craziness. She has always lived just as she wanted without worrying about a thing. Deaf as she is now and blind in one eye, she dances and laughs as though nothing were wrong. But recently her good eye has grown a lot weaker. The doctors have been telling her for a while now that she is going to lose it, too. Yesterday, in the middle of a conversation she told me, 'I have to snatch all the pleasure I can from life, and quick. I've only got one lamp still lit on the world and when it goes out, it won't be funny. No matter though, because all my precautions are taken. You think I could endure sitting around like a mummy? Not me! Oh, no, not me!' She showed me a small bottle she had hidden in a drawer. 'I've got just what I need in here,' she said, 'for me to go dancing in the other world. And the minute that I can't see the day any more — zip! The game is over. It took me nine years to fill this bottle bit by bit, but you can bet it won't take me nine seconds to empty it.' She spoke like it was the most ordinary thing in the world. Imagine. That idea has been brewing in her mind for nine years. Isn't that terrible?"

"Yes," said Fanny, "but I understand poor Irene. There are times when a person is better off dead than alive."

"Couldn't we steal her bottle from her?" asked Mrs. Lattimore.

"I wouldn't have the courage," said Fanny thoughtfully.

XLVII

Fanny slept little that night. She could not stop thinking of the meeting between Donat Sylvain and Lucy and of the new shape that things would take on Commonwealth Avenue. The furniture would certainly be rearranged; Lucy's photographs would reappear on the tables. But it was their caresses which hurt her most, the treasure that had been brutally taken from her. And Donat? He would be happy at first, but slowly he would miss the close attention that she had given him. He would not find a tie always laid out for him, his meals would not be served on time every day. He would miss the songs that he loved, also, and sometimes in spite of himself he would think of her and sigh longingly. But he would not be fool enough to break away from Lucy and come back to her.

The next morning she decided to go to a placement agency immediately. Solitude and idleness would be fatal to her. Charlie Ross was not working that day.

"Take care of things," she said. "I'll be back soon."

In fact, she was not gone long, but as she was approaching the door of her building she saw Charlie Ross come out, and turn the corner of the street. She rushed to catch up with him.

"What's going on?" she demanded. "Don't you have enough patience to wait for me?"

Charlie Ross gave her a curious look. "Somebody came to see you," he said. "He's still there. I thought the two of you could do without me."

"Somebody? Who?" asked Fanny.

"Don't ask me. A man. I've never seen him before. But he seems to know you well enough. I wasn't aware you hung around white people."

"He's white?" said Fanny. "And he knows me?"

"He certainly does. It upset him because you weren't there."

"Oh, I can guess who he is," she said, hiding her excitement. "He has come to see me on business. Thank you, Charlie. I'll leave you now."

"Yeah, I can see you're leaving me," Charlie Ross said coldly and walked off.

Fanny ran until she reached the landing in front of her apartment, then hurriedly she opened the door. Seated at the table was Donat Sylvain, the only white man who existed for her. He rose as she entered, and they both stood staring at each other, not moving.

"You? Here?" said Fanny, after a moment. "I'm so happy to see you!"

"Fanny, did you believe that we could leave each other that way?" asked Donat Sylvain.

"I thought it was the best way," said Fanny sadly. "Not to see each other, to make a complete break. But, all the same, it's good of you to come to say goodbye."

158

"Goodbye?" asked Donat Sylvain tenderly. He drew her close to him, holding her against his breast. He stroked her wet cheeks as though consoling a child. "Goodbye, you say?" he repeated, running his hand across the hair on her forehead. "Goodbye, poor Fanny." He hesitated as he spoke the word, as if he were savoring it. Then all at once he straightened up and said almost harshly.

"This little scene is very pretty, but I have no time to lose. I have to be downtown at eleven o'clock and I haven't had lunch."

His words sounded odd to Fanny and they shocked her at the same time. "Oh, excuse me," she said. "I'll fix you something."

"Good. Then I'll leave. I'm counting on you. You know the way, don't you? Above all, don't make me wait."

"What?" said Fanny. "You mean . . .?"

"Obviously, I 'mean.' Isn't it the way things usually are?"

"Then you're not going to . . .?"

"Of course not, silly fool, I'm 'not going to.' Does that surprise you?"

"But, Lucy?"

"Oh, Lucy. Charming, isn't she? We spoke for twenty minutes and she understood perfectly. She is really quite intelligent."

Fanny leapt towards the lover whom she had found again; pressing her face against his neck she cried for joy, just as she had cried as a young girl on Mr. Lewis' shoulder.

XLVIII

Donat Sylvain and Fanny were at peace now; their love had stood the test. But Charlie Ross was intrigued by Fanny's visitor.

"Who was the pale face," he asked her the same evening, "that was trying so hard to find you?"

"None of your business," said Fanny. "But if you must know, it was only the man I work for."

"Don't you go there every day? Why does he need to come around here?"

"Ask him next time, Charlie."

"Is he married, this man? Does he have a wife and kids?"

"Whether he's married or not, what difference does it make to you?"

"None at all. Well, yeah, it makes a difference to see you taking up with a white man in any way. Can't you find somebody your own color to work for?"

"That shows how much you know about Boston," said Fanny. "Do you think you choose the employer that pleases you?"

"I don't see why just because he didn't find you home he had to get so upset," said Charlie Ross.

"And I don't see why you're so worked up. Come on, be reasonable. Don't make a scene."

Nothing more was said between them, but from that moment on Charlie Ross seemed preoccupied and downcast. When Fanny returned from work he looked at her intently and it was difficult for him not to question her about the man who had so disturbed him. As well, he tried even harder to come closer to her.

"Fanny," he said, "I have a job and I act proper. I do it all for you, don't you see that?"

"Of course," said Fanny, "and it makes me very happy."

"I shouldn't be so frank, but I can say that all my life I've thought of you. Even before the day I kissed you. I've always had my eye on you from near or far, without you suspecting it. When I helped Mr. Lewis, I did it for you, and I can promise you that I was wishing he would die. When you left for Boston, I thought I'd be able to forget you. But things only got worse. Then I came to stay with you. That made me feel better. But why don't you love your old pal? You never say a sweet word to me. If you wanted me, I would be your lover. I would serve you and obey your every command. Don't be so hard on a man who loves you. You won't even give me those two kisses."

Fanny did not know what to say. She felt sorry for him, and regretted to have to hurt him, but in order not to yield, she muttered: "You're being very silly," and turned her back.

Soon after, an incident occurred which served to aggravate the tension between them. One afternoon as Fanny and Donat Sylvain were leaving a movie theater, they met George and Celia who were leaving, also. Fanny wanted desperately to avoid them, but to do so was impossible.

"Mister Sylvain," she said, halting, "here's a surprise. This is none other than George, one of my sons."

"Really?" said Donat Sylvain, shaking George's hand cordially. "The poet?"

"None other. And this is Celia, his good friend.

How is everything?'' she asked them. ''Come to see me more often. Mr. Sylvain very kindly takes me to picture shows now and then.''

''I'm glad to see you, mama,'' said George, who was as embarrassed as Fanny. ''Yes, we're doing fine. And you, you look in good health. Ah, it's too bad that we can't stay and talk. But we'll be by to see you soon.''

''All right,'' said Fanny. ''Goodbye, both of you.''

George and Celia went on and Donat Sylvain followed them with his eyes. ''Your son resembles you,'' he remarked to Fanny. ''A person would take you for his big sister. Bring him to the apartment someday. And the one who writes poetry, too.''

Fanny was bothered by this untimely encounter. She could not help wondering what its outcome would be. Then three days later, Charlie Ross went to visit George and Celia and the girl told him of the meeting.

''I wouldn't tell a soul but you,'' she began mysteriously, ''but Mrs. Lewis has a boy friend who's white! Isn't it incredible? I saw them with my own eyes leaving the Orpheum. And you would have split your sides laughing at their faces. They were smiling from ear to ear at each other. I almost fell over backwards.''

''You're sure, absolutely sure, that it was them?'' asked Charlie Ross.

''Sure? Just a little bit! George was with me. He spoke to them.''

Charlie Ross said nothing at first. He was overwhelmed by what he had heard. Then, forcing a smile he said: ''Ah! It's nothing at all. That's her boss. He's just paying her back for fixing him a good soup.'' But inwardly he was seething with anger. His suspicions were well-founded. Fanny had a lover —

white lover. Harsh, violent feelings welled within him. After Mr. Lewis, here was another hated rival to cope with. And he had always been ignored or rejected. He could not love Fanny less. On the contrary, he loved her more. He blamed the white man for having seduced her; he blamed her sons for not seeing what was happening; he blamed Celia for telling him about it; he blamed Boston — damned city! — for being a place where such things could occur. "Now, Fanny has got to listen to me," he said to himself.

To give himself even crueler proof, he followed Fanny secretly for several days. From afar he watched as she entered the apartment on Commonwealth Avenue with its windows full of flowers. The beauty of the boulevard, which was lined on both sides with trees, the luxurious appearance of the house which Fanny entered, pierced him like thorns. "It's because he's rich," Charlie Ross thought. "Rich people can buy whatever they want. But she doesn't really love him. She'll come back to me."

He would wait for Fanny until late in the afternoon, expecting to see her come out of the house with her lover. Finally, one evening they appeared together. Fanny was wearing a dress he had never seen. She was trim and smiling, so much the young girl he had known in Greenway. Beside her, smart and attentive, was the light-skinned man whom he knew only too well. The sight filled him with hatred which was difficult to master. He would have liked to pounce upon this man who dared covet a forbidden woman, stolen from her people and her true friends. He let them go unmolested, however, and started back towards Shawmut Avenue with his head down. While on his way there he stopped in a bar and did not leave until he was drunker than he had ever been in his life.

163

IL

Irene's condition grew much worse. She was practically cut off from the outside world. She was now completely deaf and she did not know how to read lips. It was necessary to write her notes in order to communicate with her, but still she had difficulty reading them, for the pupil of her remaining eye was clouded over with an opaque film, and crowded with white spots which made it almost impossible for her to see, and the eye caused her great pain. The salve given her free of charge by the hospital relieved her for an hour or so, but then it was necessary to reapply it. No longer able to have a job, she depended on the state for food and money, receiving a check for an absurdly low sum each week.

There was no one on whom she could depend. She did not know if her father was dead or alive. He had abandoned her when she was still a child, leaving her only the legacy of his impure blood from which she now suffered. Her mother, a devoted but harsh woman, had been dead a long time. If she had brothers and sisters, they were dispersed throughout the United States. From the time that she was sixteen, she had moved from one city to another, working as a servant, a chambermaid, a children's nurse, a washerwoman a cook, seeing every kind of person in every milieu. She had always been cheerful, intrepid and violent She refused neither a wild party nor a furious argument, and she was capable of happy laughter and sharp retorts. Her employers retained her because of her honesty and intelligence. She made them smile with her sallies, but they learned quickly to handle her with tact.

She had had countless lovers, attracted both by her lovely figure and her spirit, but not one of them had ever ruled her. They followed her lead; she determined the limits of every relationship. She was, as they say, a "character," dangerously explosive but attractive and friendly in many ways. Now at thirty-six her primitive vitality was checked. She could hardly see the world and she could not hear it at all. But inside her prison she remained undaunted. No one knew her thoughts, but in front of others she was active and uncomplaining. She still laughed and exchanged barbs, and she seemed, at least, to forget her wretched circumstances at the slightest pretext. She still had the poison which she was to take when she became totally blind, and she spoke of it indifferently as though it were nothing unusual.

Secretly she suffered from not having enough money to buy herself the elegant clothes and shoes that she once wore. Her dresses, most of them gifts, were plain and, according to her, they gave her the look of a matron or a deaconess. She had a special dislike for her glass eye. "Looks like a doll's eye," she said, "and even some dolls' eyes move around in their heads." She told Fanny confidentially: "Would you believe it? They make false eyes now that move. Yes ma'am, with little hooks that latch on to your nerves and do what your nerves want them to. But they're awful expensive — twelve or fifteen dollars. I said to myself: 'Irene, you just keep looking straight ahead with your old dead fish's eyeball.' Oh, ho!" she guffawed, "Lawrence says I scare him."

Fanny repeated Irene's words to her neighbors. They all felt sorry for her in spite of the fact that she did not want their pity, and they did everything they could for her. Then Fanny had an idea. "Irene wants a glass eye that moves," she said to Maude Olliver. "What if we got together and bought her one?" Mrs. Rollins and Mrs. Lattimore agreed eagerly. Each of them put aside twenty-five cents a week and Lawrence and other men were made to donate some money. To the last, Irene suspected nothing. Edward was delegated to find out what he could about the eye and its cost. In less that eight weeks they had collected the amount of money needed. Soon Irene was presented with a receipt signed by a well-known optometrist "good for one movable glass eye." Tenderness was not a part of Irene's make-up. She showed her gratitude with boisterous laughter and by giving her neighbors smothering embraces.

Frank drove her to the optometrist's office for the first measurements. Several tests and changes were necessary, but soon her new eye matched her other perfectly. She returned from her last visit in triumph. The eye was an artistic marvel, so natural that it seemed alive. Like its twin it moved up and down and from side to side. In minutes everyone in the building had heard of the wonder and they found excuses to come admire it. With a crowd around her, Irene looked at herself in a mirror; then she turned her gaze upon the group. "This eye's the better of the two," she declared. "I've a mind to trade the other one for one just like it." Lawrence handed her a note which read: "I'm not afraid of you any more." She turned towards him with both eyes flashing and gave him a resounding slap.

One month later, however, Irene became totally

blind. Maude Olliver went to see her one morning and found her dead in her bed. At her side was the small bottle, empty except for some traces of a green powder.

L

If Charlie Ross had been better acquainted with the customs of Boston, he would not have been so surprised by Fanny's relationship with Donat Sylvain. In Boston, attachments of the kind were not rare. Even in Roxbury, had he noticed, he could have seen numerous mixed marriages, and a larger number of love affairs between blacks and whites to which few paid any attention. Throughout the country, in spite of taboos, and even in the time of slavery, a secret attraction existed between the two races. Gradually, the races are coming together. Already in certain areas there are more "blond Africans" than Negroes who hardly show a trace of their ancestry, suggesting for some later date an automatic and highly ironic solution to "the black problem."

But statistics were not sufficient to calm the bitterness eating away at Charlie Ross' heart. This was his own problem, and it concerned the woman he loved and who rightfully belonged to him. The thought of her together with her white man was like a nightmare. He argued with her every day. "Aren't you ashamed of betraying your own color like this?" he'd say. "Your grandmother was their slave. Do you want to be one, too? What would your friends in Greenway think? What would Mr. Lewis think?'' Then seeing that his arguments had no effect on Fanny, he changed his tune. Had she forgotten what she and he had shared together, he asked. The affection that he had had for her so many years? Where would she ever find a friend as devoted and as obedient as he? He said the same thing day after day, and Fanny found him difficult to bear.

Fanny's sons knew nothing of what was happening between her and Charlie Ross. But one evening when the four of them were home, Charlie Ross decided to speak out.

''Young men,'' he said, ''what do you think of a black woman who falls in love with a white man? They say that things like that happen.''

''Goodness,'' said Frank, after thinking a moment, ''it depends on the situation. If they really love each other, I'd say it was their business.''

''Well, that's not the way I think,'' said Edward. ''White people humiliate us in enough ways without stealing our girls. If black girls had a little pride . . .''

''That's a good way to think,'' Charlie Ross interrupted. ''And you, Fanny, what do you think?''

Fanny felt the blood rush to her cheeks. It was insolent of him to speak that way in front of her sons. Would she be trapped? ''I'll let you argue it out among yourselves,'' she said coldly. ''I know what I think.'' But immediately after she had spoken she thought it cowardly not to defend her feelings. Why should she be afraid? Provocatively, she continued: ''If you want to know, a woman loves whoever pleases her. Her heart tells her whom to love. All barriers are useless; they're only made to be jumped. White, black, yellow or copper, we're all men and women with nothing but

168

different colors between us; we're all God's children. If they decide to come together they don't have to account to anybody, and it's not you, Charlie Ross, who'll stop them.''

The two brothers looked at each other, surprised by their mother's decided tone. Charlie Ross had been silenced. He did not dare continue the discussion. ''Don't be too sure,'' he grumbled. ''There are some things that we have a right to stop.''

LI

''What was Charlie's outburst all about, mama?'' asked Frank the next morning. ''After you went to sleep, he didn't want to say another word.''

''Don't let it upset you,'' said Fanny with a nervous laugh. ''Charlie Ross is like that. He has his principles.''

''Mama, answer me seriously. Does Charlie bother you?''

''Yes, he does. You see how close he stays to me. But I can put up with it, and I'm not afraid of him.''

''But, I don't want anyone to bother you,'' said Frank. ''I'm going to tell him to move.''

''Don't do that, Frank. You'll make him very angry. And what he said, you know, doesn't make the least impression on me.''

''But I can see that he suspects you of something. Can you tell me what it is?''

She hesitated a moment before speaking: ''He suspects that I'm in love with the man I work for, Mister Sylvain. And he's absolutely right," she added candidly. "It's a fact that I love him."

She had spoken simply, without boasting. She waited for her son's response.

"Oh, is that it?" said Frank calmly. "Poor mama," he added, putting his arms around her. "I had sort of guessed it. Do you think it shocks me? You're young and beautiful. You have the right to love whoever you want. I'd like to see someone try to stop you."

"Then you understand?" said Fanny. "You don't hold it against me?"

"I'm on your side, mama: today, tomorrow and always."

"I'm grateful to you, Frank. In that case, try to explain to Charlie so he'll leave me alone. But go slowly. He's very stubborn."

Edward, also, had thought about the incident. He went to Fanny when, as usual, she was addressing copies of the *Exchange*, and said, "Mother I'm sorry if I seemed to be against you. But you were joking with Charlie Ross, weren't you? In accepting that black women . . ."

"No, Edward, I was serious. I said exactly what I thought."

"Come now, mama, that's impossible! Think of the tyranny that keeps our people down. If our women betray us..."

"Betray? I call it serving us. Even from your point of view. It's infiltrating the enemy, breaking him, mastering him, putting him at your mercy. That's what every black woman does, dear child, who's loved by a white man. You knew your Bible once. Think of Delilah," she said half laughing and half sincere.

"Well, if that's the way you see it," said Edward, confounded. "But I know you're joking, all the same."

"Think what you like," Fanny concluded, "but beware of jokes. They have the truth in them a lot of times." She could see that she had not changed his mind. Obviously, he could only see one side of the argument; he would never understand the other. She could not hope ever to take him into her confidence.

LII

"Listen," said Frank to Charlie Ross when they were alone, "you're a good guy and we all like you; but you should watch the way you act sometimes."

"What do you mean, boy?" asked Charlie Ross, surprised.

"I mean with mama. You follow behind her a little closer than you have to. I'm sorry, but it gets on her nerves."

Charlie Ross started as though stuck by a needle. "It gets on her nerves?" he repeated. "Did she say to tell me that?"

"She didn't have to," said Frank. "I've got eyes to see."

"What do you see? Am I forward or vulgar around your mama?"

"Oh, it's not that. But no matter . . . you ought to understand that she doesn't like to be tormented. You

171

try her patience talking about that white man all the time.''

''So you know about her white man, too. And you don't mind? You don't think it's shameful?''

''Shameful? Why? In any case, it's neither my nor anybody else's business. Mama's not a child. She knows what she's doing.''

''If you'd grown up with your mother like I did,'' said Charlie Ross, ''and seen what kind of girl she was, it would burn you up, too, to see her stoop so low.''

''She's not lowering herself,'' said Frank, angered. ''Don't use that word when you speak about her.'' He and Charlie Ross glared at each other. ''It would be much simpler'' Frank continued, restraining himself, ''if you weren't around her so much. Things would be quieter and we could remain friends.''

Incensed, Charlie Ross screamed: ''Does she want me to leave? Is she throwing me out?''

''Nobody's forcing you. I'm asking you. It's my idea. I live here, after all.''

Charlie Ross hesitated a moment, trembling with silent rage. ''Fine. I'll leave,'' he said finally, between his teeth. ''But nothing will stop me from speaking to your mother and from tearing her away from that white man. Damn it, I'll kill him if it's the only way!''

''Don't say stupid things,'' said Frank. ''It doesn't get you anywhere.''

LIII

"He's gone," Frank informed his mother that same evening. "He wasn't too pleased, but I was determined. Only watch out, he's still ready to bother you."

"I can stand it," said Fanny, "if it's not every day. Thank you, Frank, you're my good friend. Do you know where he went?"

"No. George's, I imagine."

Fanny wondered if Charlie Ross would turn her son against her. She was relieved by his departure, but she was not entirely reassured. She foresaw that she would have to fight for her love. At least Donat knew nothing of the trouble Charlie Ross was causing, and she would not disturb him with her own problems.

"He's at George's," announced Frank a short time later, "and I learned that he's sulking. He's quit work and he drinks all the time. He'll get over it, naturally, but you'd do well to avoid him for a while, mother."

"Whatever you avoid, Frank, will get you in the end. I don't feel the need to hide from Charlie Ross. If he speaks to me, I'll answer him. I don't blame him for anything. And I know how to handle him."

LIV

That day and those following she went as usual to Donat Sylvain's house. She regretted making Charlie Ross unhappy, but Donat was her lover; she forgot about the world when she was with him.

Donat Sylvain was unaware of any threat to their peaceful life. Each day revealed yet another unforeseen charm of this childlike woman, and strengthened the bond which held them together.

Their different lives had come together in a unique combination made up of the most varied elements of their natures: simplicity and culture, experience and naivete, reserve and rashness, gaiety and melancholy, calm tenderness and ardent passion. Even their disputes brought them closer together, as though they were no more than games.

"Do you know how this will end?" asked Donat Sylvain. "One fine day I'm going to marry you."

"Oh, no," Fanny replied, "you don't know what you're saying. Marry me and lower yourself in the eyes of your friends? Do you see yourself presenting me to your high-class friends, 'My wife, Mrs. Donat Sylvain.'"

"I don't care about those friends," he said insistently. "If they don't want you then they can do without me, too. I would like them to know my contempt for their stupid caste system."

"You fool," said Fanny, covering his face with kisses. "You're my husband just as you are."

174

It was difficult for Fanny to say those words. Nothing would have made her happier than to be Donat Sylvain's wife; the idea was beyond her wildest dreams. But she could not forget the differences in their races. It was a barrier which had withstood the bravest challenges. She could not dismiss the thought of her love's future, of Edward and George, and, vaguely, of Charlie Ross.

"Buy me a wedding ring," she said, "a beautiful wedding ring as though we were really married, and I'll promise to be yours forever. That will take the place of a licence."

"Serve as one in the meantime," Donat Sylvain said after a moment. "But I won't forget what I said. I tell you that one of these days I'll drag you before a minister and marry you, whether you want it or not."

He brought her an expensive ring mounted with diamonds and placed it on her finger. Then, filled with a strange emotion, they repeated the marriage vow to each other. "In sickness and in health, for richer and for poorer, in joy and in sorrow, for better or for worse, till death us do part."

LV

Fanny, having come early to Donat Sylvain's apartment, was singing as she did her day's work. Donat Sylvain was in his study with the door closed, for he had received an important commission, and when he could see or hear Fanny, he could think only of her. Fanny sang softly in order not to disturb him. For the time being she was in the kitchen, which was separated from his study by two rooms. Her heart was light. She was still excited by the pact that she had made with her lover. The sunlight on the window-panes reminded her of the happy times of her life: her youthful wanderings across Greenway's fields, the spirited games at school, the charm of her first love.

She was roused from her daydreams by a knock at the door. "Why don't these salesmen ring first?" she thought. She laid her basket of vegetables aside and went to answer the door. When she opened it she found Charlie Ross standing in front of her. She stepped back instinctively and tried to close the door, but Charlie placed his foot in the doorway.

"What do you want?" she asked, looking nervously at the closed door of Donat Sylvain's study. "Keep your voice down so no one can hear you."

"I came to see you," said Charlie Ross, "and to talk to you. You've got to listen to me, Fanny."

"But not here, Charlie, not while I'm working. Come to my place some night and talk to me."

"No. It's got to be here and now. Let me in."

He pushed the door open with his shoulder. The unusual gleam in his eyes told her that he had been drinking, but he was not drunk. His step was firm and his voice was even and steady. He was being driven by a desperate but conscious resolve.

Fanny anxiously tried to think of a way to avoid a scene and keep Donat Sylvain from knowing of Charlie Ross' presence. But the latter was determined. She had to think fast. There was only one way, she would talk to him, humor him.

"Well, come in for a moment," she said, "but don't make any noise. This isn't my house, you know. Really, you shouldn't have surprised me like this."

They went into the kitchen. Fanny closed all the doors leading to the rest of the apartment.

"You wanted to see where I work? Nothing out of the ordinary, do you think? It's just like any other kitchen. It's where I try to earn my living. But it's not a place where you can stand around and talk. Be nice, go back home; and tonight I'll speak to you as long as you like."

"Don't try to make a fool of me," said Charlie Ross bitterly. "You know why I've come."

"But, I don't. How could I?" she protested.

"I want to know, yes or no: are you going to give up this white man and come back with us, with your own kind? Answer me right now."

Fanny was angered by Charlie Ross' presumption, but she did not dare show it fully. "You don't have any right to ask me such a question," she said. "Don't be so insolent, I beg you, and leave me alone!"

"It's for your own good," Charlie Ross insisted. "I love you, you know that; and I want you. But, by God, if I can't have you, no damned stranger will. Your lover's here. Lead me to him and we'll have it

177

out right now."

Fanny was about to answer him sharply, but she stopped, transfixed by the sight of an object protruding from the pocket of his coat. Reflecting the kitchen's light was the steel sheath of a razor, the treacherous and favorite weapon of black people, wielded like lightning in their fatal brawls. Fanny felt a sudden terror. Charlie Ross was going to use his razor against her lover. In his possessed state he would stop at nothing. He would provoke a quarrel with Donat and kill him before he could defend himself, and she would be the cause of his death. Her only thought was to save him from Charlie Ross at any cost.

"You take things too seriously, Charlie," she said cajolingly. "Who told you that I love this white man and that I've forgotten about my old pals? You're dreaming. Do you believe that I don't think often of those days, of you and our old friends? Here, I'll make a deal with you. You know those two kisses I've owed you for so long? If you will calm down, I'll pay my debt. That's a good deal, isn't it; two kisses, right here? And then afterwards, will you do as I ask?"

As though by magic, Fanny's words distracted Charlie Ross from his obsession. He hesitated, seduced by the mirage of a joy which he had sought for so long, and which finally seemed to be within his reach. He appeared to relax, and his silence gave his consent, spoke his willingness to pay the price demanded for this miracle.

Fanny walked towards him and placed an arm around his neck. Then she pressed her cheek against his lips. She had charmed him, and while he gave himself up to the pleasure of her embrace, she placed her other arm alongside his body and insinuated her hand imperceptibly into the pocket where the razor lay. She

178

touched it, but at that instant Charlie Ross felt the furtive movement of her fingers, and knew after a single puzzled moment what she was attempting to do.

"You traitor! You slut!" he shouted. "So that's what you wanted!"

They grappled fiercely and desperately together; each had a hold on the razor. They stumbled and rolled on the floor, fighting silently with their teeth tightly clenched, just as they had fought in the shadow of the chestnut tree. During one of their violent turns the razor opened, and without suspecting it Charlie Ross pressed it against Fanny's wrist. Blood began to spurt from a deep wound. "Stop!" Fanny moaned, "you've hurt me." But Charlie Ross, deaf with rage and the pain of betrayal, did not hear her. The weight of his body lay full upon the razor, pushing it farther into Fanny's wrist. Not until he felt the warmth of her blood upon the palm of his hand did he realize what had happened.

"What's the matter?" he said, alarmed. Then he saw the blackish pool underneath them. "God! What have I done?" he cried, leaping to his feet. "I've hurt you, Fanny. I've cut you. I didn't know. Oh, no, I didn't want that. Tell me what to do. How can I help you? Jesus, not this!"

He stood helpless, almost hysterical. Fanny raised herself up slightly. As though in a trance she looked at the blood flowing from her arm. She felt very weak.

"Do just as I tell you," she said. "First, take the razor and put it back in your pocket. Take a rag from that drawer and tie it around my wrist. Then take that knife on the table and put it near me in the blood. Then wash your hands and throw the paper towel in the fireplace. Afterwards, leave this apartment and don't ever come back. Once outside, telephone a doctor, any one, and send him here. And, above all, don't say a word to anybody."

"Fanny," said Charlie Ross sobbing, "I can't leave you like this. Let me put you on a bed."

"You have to obey me," said Fanny. "You got your two kisses, you know."

Full of tears, Charlie Ross hastily and nervously did as Fanny instructed. But before leaving, he said: "Will you ever forgive me?"

"I already have, Charlie. I don't blame you for anything. It's an accident, nothing else. Otherwise, don't think you would have gotten the best of me. But if you want to know what I think, Charlie, I think you should go back to the South as soon as you can."

"Don't worry about me, my love. The only thing on my mind right now is to get you some help." Charlie Ross turned and hurried from the apartment. When he reached the staircase he began to run.

Alone, Fanny was aware of the seriousness of her wound. Her blood continued to flow; it showed through the cloth of her bandage. She felt intense pain and could hardly move. Would she die here, she wondered, from loss of blood? At least Donat was safe. He would never know of the danger that had been so close to him. This thought gave her some peace.

LVI

Fanny lay quietly on her hospital bed, weak and unmoving. Donat Sylvain had come out of his study moments after Charlie Ross left the apartment and discovered her crawling towards him, leaving a trail of blood behind her. He had rushed over to her, horrified. "What happened to you, Fanny?" he asked.

"While I was cutting vegetables," she murmured weakly, "I fell on the knife. But I called a doctor; he's coming." Then she lost consciousness.

When the doctor arrived soon after, Sylvain was beside himself with grief. He had carried Fanny to the couch and, kneeling beside her, he was kissing her tenderly and begging her to wake up. The doctor quickly called an ambulance and she was taken to the nearest first-aid station. "It's a serious case," said the intern. "An artery has been cut. The young woman has lost a lot of blood." She revived, however, enough to look around her, searching for a familiar face. She smiled when she saw Donat Sylvain, who took her hand in silence. Her sons were notified and came to her side where they stood rigid with shock. The tenants on Sawmut Avenue were in turmoil. They commented profusely on what they considered to be a strange accident, and spoke warmly of their neighbor. Fanny, stretched out on her bed, was too weak to undergo any violent shock. Her mind swam in a tranquil fog; she lay in the repose of one whose life hung by a thread. But her heart remembered. She

181

looked softly at Donat Sylvain, and at Edward, Frank and George, and mumbled hopeful words. Then the four were asked to leave so that she could rest. She was left alone behind the curtain surrounding her bed, with only her nurses staying with her. They would have to wait until the next day to see her again.

LVII

During the night, thanks to the medicine she was given and to a deep sleep, Fanny regained some strength, but she remained in serious condition. It was thought that a blood transfusion might save her, so a search was begun for blood of the same type as hers.

Donat Sylvain did not sleep. The following morning his face was ashen and his mind heavy with the horror of the nightmare through which he was living. The surrounding world had lost all reality; Fanny was suffering, struggling for her life. Intolerable terror filled his heart when he thought of losing her; it was a thought as maddening as the end of the universe.

Another man, also, walked the floor of the hospital in despair. He had been there for several hours constantly inquiring about Fanny's condition. He was asked what relation he was to the patient. He was her best friend, he answered. Finally, he demanded: "Is there anything I can do for her?"

"Give a pint of blood," came the reply.

"Take it all, if you want it," he cried.

Then he was led to Fanny's room. She recognized

Charlie Ross. She was surprised at first, but after a few moments she smiled at him sadly. "Not a word to anybody," she whispered. While the blood of her old friend flowed into Fanny's veins, Donat Sylvain entered the room. He thanked him, thinking that he was expressing gratitude to a stranger for his service. Charlie Ross noticed the way in which Fanny and Donat Sylvain looked at each other and he understood the strength of the love that was between them.

LVIII

Another long and anguishing night passed during which Fanny lay half-conscious and Donat Sylvain sat brooding over the tragedy which threatened. He and Maude Olliver happened to visit Fanny at the same time. She recognized them and saw that they were crying. The sight of them consoled her, and she was touched by their tears. She summoned her strength and spoke: "Dearest," she said to Donat Sylvain, "if I die, you'll need another housekeeper. A black woman, maybe? To remember me? You would like Maude. She's my best friend. She's more serious than I am, but she's a wonderful person." Donat Sylvain felt choked with sorrow before such devotion and selfless renunciation.

LIX

In spite of the doctor's efforts, Fanny weakened rapidly. Between her moments of pain the impetuous young girl who had never grown old would speak quietly, but feverishly and incoherently like an aged person in her second childhood, of times and persons in her life, Linda, Mr. Lewis, her four sons, Charlie Ross, Donat Sylvain floated dreamlike through her thoughts. "Mr. Lewis, I liked you very much, I threw pillows at you. Oh, but you had Martha Bledsoe, who was much nicer than I was. Come, go to sleep Frank, George, Robert, Edward, my dear little boys. Once upon a time. Tick-tock, bluebird, all blue. Honestly. I feel so sleepy, but I have to go apologize to my employer, to finish my work at Mr. Sylvain's. This kitchen is a mess. It's too bad that the knife scratched me. Children shouldn't be allowed to play with knives Now I'm going to bed for at least a week. Who wil do your work then, Mr. Sylvain? But I'll come back to you. Pray to Father Divine for me to come back to you. Peace — it's wonderful. This time I promise you that I won't ever leave you again, my dearest For better or worse, till death do us part. Swing low sweet chariot, coming along, coming along. Tick tock, tick-tock, tick.''

LX

Following each of these attacks Fanny lay quietly, weakened and unmoving. She was vaguely conscious of what was happening around her, smiling at her sons and friends. Each time Donat Sylvain leaned over her, pressing her hand lovingly in silence, her face brightened and their tearful looks expressed the unity of their minds and hearts.

Emaciated, almost ethereal, even in defeat Fanny's body kept its indestructible youth. Her face had taken on a new, purer beauty, the reflection of her virginal soul. Patience and tranquil resignation were there, too. She was accepting her ultimate trial as simply as she had accepted all others. She had reached the tragic summit, where destiny, through the byways of her commonplace life, had led her.

LXI

During the night, Fanny died. The nurse assigned to her bedside saw her tremble violently and attempt to sit up. With clouded eyes she scanned the room, as if searching for her loved ones. "I want to get out o here," she cried. "I have work to do!" Then she fel back, her life gone. Even though those whom she ha sought were not with her at the moment of her death they had not abandoned her. Their hands were joine in a final effort to pull her away from the precipice to safety. But Fanny died in spite of them, and the learned of love's impotence against destiny. For th hospital, the young woman's death was an ordinar occurrence. The white curtains around her bed wer drawn; the nursing sister sprinkled a few last drop of holy water over her. But for a small group o people this senseless, unforeseen event was a misfor tune which no amount of mourning could assuage an irreparable disaster which struck at the center their hearts; between them and her, the definitiv separation. With this small lamp's flame snuffed ou the world was left in darkness.

But here the story of her death becomes that of a deaths. Why follow it further? Why discuss the regr and deep despair that this obscure African leav behind her? For a few moments out of all eterni she came as others come to smile, to sing, to devo herself, to love and to be loved. What importan have the rites which will sanctify her remains, or t preacher's formula of words? The lovely procession which will carry her away, self-righteously, as though in triumph, or the isolated corner of the cemetery in which she will lie? What importance has the existence of her friends who will continue to live? Their world disappeared with her. Never again will their lives be the same. Weary, as after a night of terrible dreams, they will have to resume the burden of their days. At first the routine will seem senseless and unbearable, a feeling of emptiness will haunt them continually. Then time will slowly ease their pain. They will never forget, but their sadness will be replaced by the sweetness of memories. They will live, suffer other torments, and think in their turn of their own deaths.

One among them, perhaps, will never recover. Fanny will stay with him as a tragic ghost, a soul, more than a mere memory; always at his side, eternally young, accompanying him wherever life leads him — and yet, forever lost.